MUNSTER VILLAGE

Lady Mary Hamilton was born in Edinburgh in 1739, the youngest daughter of Elizabeth and Alexander Leslie, the Countess and Earl of Leven and Melville. She married Dr James Walker in 1762; after his death, she married Robert Hamilton, with whom she settled in France before the Revolution. When her second husband died, she moved to Amiens with her two daughters. Lady Mary Hamilton wrote five novels, *Letters from the Duchess de Crui* (1776), *Memoirs of the Marchioness de Louvoi* (1777), *Munster Village* (1778), *The Life of Mrs Justman* (1782) and the *Duc de Popoli* (1810) – all of which show considerable erudition and campaign for women's rights to education. Lady Mary Hamilton died in 1816.

Sarah Baylis was born in 1956 in London, where she has lived all her life. She went to Sussex University, then worked as a community worker, cleaner, artist's model and cook. She is now a freelance writer and illustrator, the author of *Utrillo's Mother* (Pandora Press, 1987) and two novels for teenagers: *Vila* (Brilliance Books, 1984), winner of the Other Award for children's fiction, and *The Tomb of Reeds* (Julia McRae, 1987).

MOTHERS OF THE NOVEL
Reprint fiction from Pandora Press

Pandora is reprinting eighteenth and nineteenth century novels written by
women. Each novel is being reset into contemporary typography and
reintroduced to readers today by contemporary women novelists.
The following titles in this series are currently available:

The companion to this exciting series is:
MOTHERS OF THE NOVEL
100 Good Women Writers before Jane Austen
by Dale Spender

In this wonderfully readable survey, Dale Spender reclaims the many women
writers who made a significant contribution to the literary tradition. She
describes the interconnections among the writers, their approach and the public
response to their work.

MUNSTER VILLAGE

MARY HAMILTON

Introduced by

Sarah Baylis

PANDORA

London and New York

First published in 1987 by
Pandora Press
(Routledge & Kegan Paul Ltd)
11 New Fetter Lane, London EC4P 4EE

Published in the USA by
Pandora Press
(Routledge & Kegan Paul Inc.)
in association with Methuen Inc.
29 West 35th Street, New York, NY 10001

Set in 10 on 11½ pt Ehrhardt
by Columns of Reading
and printed in the British Isles
by The Guernsey Press Co. Ltd
Guernsey, Channel Islands

Library of Congress Cataloging in Publication Data

Hamilton, Mary, 1739-1816.
Munster Village.

(Mothers of the novel)
I. Title. II. Series.
PR3506.H38M86 1987   823'.6   86-16921

British Library CIP Data also available

ISBN 0-86358-133-1

CONTENTS

———————•———————

INTRODUCTION

———————•———————

If you fancy going to the British Library to find out about Lady Mary Hamilton, forget it. I had a go, and got nowhere (and I refuse on principle to look up her father and husbands to pick round their biographies for scraps).

So, all I know is as follows: she was born in Edinburgh in 1739, married at twenty three, was widowed, then married again, and with her second husband fled Georgian England in favour of France, where she settled in the years leading up to the Revolution. With Robert Hamilton she had two daughters, then moved to Amiens in her second widowhood. She had a poem written, by a neighbour, to the death of her favourite bullfinch. She wrote five novels, one of which was translated into French.

The youngest daughter of the fifth Earl of Levin, she would have been lucky and rich enough to receive a certain kind of education – the usual thing: music, painting, deportment etc. as well as learning how to be a successful 'society' woman. (Very important, and not to be underestimated: a man may ignore society and become a rake, but a woman can't.) However the usual education suitable for a woman wasn't designed to make her a novelist: there must be a far greater thirst for that to take place, and we can assume that any woman of great cultivation had to work hard to gain her learning.

It's hard for us to imagine the constrictions for women in the second half of the eighteenth century. A poor woman was simply a slave – doubly so, for she belonged to one man (father, husband or brother) who in turn belonged to the Master. The rich woman also belonged, as often as not, to a man. She had leisure, perhaps, but a deadly leisure that stifled her so that '... she is often sick without knowing *where* her complaint *lies*, because she has nothing to *do*, and is tired of being *well*.' All our images of this time come from literature, paintings and history books, but which image do we believe: the gouty crush of Hogarth's *Rake's Progress*, the caricatures of Cruikshank, and the bawdyness of Henry Fielding? Or the untroubled cleanliness of the pink-ribboned women of Sir Joshua Reynolds, and the weighty moralising of Samuel Richardson? Certainly, urban life was very different from genteel country existence; but to an extent, upper-class women were in neither world seen as much more than ornamental – useful vessels for vices and virtues that were thrust upon them but seldom chosen.

In *Munster Village* we glimpse both worlds. Slung loosely upon the bones of a plot that follows the fortunes of two generations of the Munster family, weaving standard problems around a series of lovers, is a portrait of eighteenth-century England as it was observed by a woman of intellect and erudition. (If Lady Frances is not modelled on Lady Mary Hamilton herself, I'm sure she's modelled on how she wished, in some way, to be.) She creates for us – within the confines of a conventional novel (which in 1778 when this work first appeared, was a form newborn indeed) – a place of learning and beauty that would shine as a jewel, lighting the way from ignorance and folly towards enlightenment. And she's not unconscious of her unashamed basking in the glories of neo-classicism, but lampoons the love affair with Renaissance Italy of Mr Harris, who 'could sit all day in contemplation of a statue with no nose'. Indeed, Lady Frances 'was advised to call her elegant village by the name of *Athens;* but this she declined, naming it *Munster Village:* but she justly thought it deserved it . . .'

Munster Village is a remarkable place; a centre for science and the arts, with nothing left out; and for every two hundred scholars admitted to the academy, a full twenty of these will be young ladies! (Modern women may quibble at a mere ten percent, but this only shows us what modest demands form the original roots of feminism.) Unemployment is solved, poverty dealt with: this is philanthropy at its most heartfelt – no radical reforms (despite the enclosure acts that throughout this most cruel of centuries were tearing rural Britain apart; despite the fact that Adam Smith's *Wealth of Nations* was fast becoming a bible for the eager proto-capitalist) but a caring and *educating* approach to land ownership – dare I say 'maternalism'? – a curiously female vision, right down to the inclusion of 'a receptable for all sorts of animals to retire to in their old age.' Lady Frances considers that 'society is manifestly maintained by a circulation of kindness: we are all of us, in some way or other, wanting assistance, and in like manner qualified to give it.' Assistance is a matter of life and death: talented artist Lady Finlay (the sweet Miss Burt) perishes 'for want of proper assistance. *Assistance*!' while struggling to support her family. It may not be a revolutionary philosophy, but it's nice to hear it voiced in a century where 'assistance' is once again being denigrated as a soft option.

Lady Frances' eutopian village may seem to be a stifling place (there's nothing democratic about her ordering of the world) but the outside does intrude through the letters of the young ones as they pass through Europe, get captured and thrown into chains as galley-slaves, languish honourably over loved ones, or go to town for the dreadful London season. The delightful details of the sheep from Norway, the corn from India, the silkworms, and the buffaloes that draw the ploughs, keep the worthiness of the novel from becoming oppressive. This is not the narrow circle that was to be favoured by Jane Austen; here we have a writer of broad scope, and if anything she makes the mistake of wanting to leave nothing unsaid: nothing is safe from her proverbs.

Lady Francis is not the only woman of strong character who has to survive on her own; *Munster Village* is full of them. There is Mrs Lee, that uncultivated jewel, 'nature itself, without disguise, quite original disdaining all imitation', who separates from her libertine husband, and mutters about divorce; there is the Duchess de Salis, also married to an unfeeling monster, another bene-factress, who establishes 'an institution for the provision of the infirm and destitute'; and there is the lovely Miss Harris, unmarried mother and mouthpiece for the sanctity of marriage and the possibility of living nobly outside that worthy institution. These women are on their own because of marriage breakdown or desertion, and certainly most of the men come out of it poorly, addicted to pleasure and reluctant to face up to their respon-sibilities. In *Munster Village* it is the women who are the educators of the young; it is they who *feel* for the less fortunate, they who *act*. They are aware that it is 'what is called pleasure, that sunk into ruin the ancient states of Greece; that destroyed the Romans, that corrupts courts, consumes youth; that has a retinue composed of satiety, indigence, sickness, and death.'

Don't forget: fine ladies in the eighteenth century may have worn ludicrous cork-inflated hairdoes and dresses that wedged them in doorways; they may have deformed themselves in stays which caused miscarriage and still-birth; but they also ran the famous salons of London and Paris that were the centres of European 'civilisation'. They may not have been encouraged, but they were *allowed* to be intelligent – as long as they did not wholly desert the domestic sphere. And Lady Mary Hamilton wasn't about to exort them to do any such thing; the domestic sphere would be safe in no other hands, and in reply to Mrs Lee's remarks on the nullity of her marriage, Lady Frances quietly refers her to certain passages in scripture 'which I think on sober reflection must invalidate your present opinion.'

Lady Mary Hamilton is not averse to the use of the homily. Everything is subject to the same pious scrutiny; all conduct is questioned, especially the conduct of men towards women, and of women on their own. The same scrutiny is given to the education of the young, and the terrible folly of the fashionable world where 'the curls of the *head* are more attended to, than the sensations of the heart.' And throughout all of this comes the same steady voice, moral but not entirely without humour. What saves the author from waxing dull and sensorious is her commitment to that 'most useful of all sciences, human nature.' (If human nature is a science, does that then mean that it is perfectible; or like science, does ultimate analysis evade even the wisest amongst us?) She may have a useful proverb for every occasion, but she speaks them with a gentle tongue, strewing her prose with references to Dr Johnson, Rousseau, Hobbs and Pliny; and guiding her reader at times to solemn footnotes: **See Bacon on government ... *see Duhalde's description of China ...* and even **see the Fifth Commandment ...*!

The author gives in completely to her love of letters in the final pages when Lord Darnley, the husband who waited patiently while Lady Frances puts her village to rights and oversees to perfection the education of her wards, throws a spectacular masque to celebrate their wedding anniversary. Enter the lights of the ancient world, the artists of the Renaissance, a few worthy Englishmen, and finally Ossain himself, with a blast of Celtic ballad. All give praise to letters, to industry and to the mistress of both, the wise Lady Frances.

Lady Mary Hamilton must have looked about her and seen women whose intellects were as constricted as their rib cages, and so she determined to speak out against it. Nothing was as repugnant to her as idleness, and she knew that 'pleasure is to be purchased, and that industry is the price of it.' This is not a lesson that ever needs to be taught to any but the most leisured and privileged (everyone else is too busy to bother) but it was leisured men and women for whom Lady Mary Hamilton was writing – the others couldn't read.

Munster Village is an invaluable document, as well as a fine novel. When you've read it you'll want to dig out your old history text books and remind yourself of the horrors of our British heritage. The records of female experience are few and far between and naturally they have been marginalised, trivialised and lost; but they still have a lot to contribute to our understanding of women's history. While contemporary feminism threatens to fragment around issues of gender and sexual difference, it's salutary and enjoyable, through re-reading these early writings by serious women, to return to a study of our earliest roots when men and women's differences were no more innate than they are today, but oh, how much more stringently enforced?

Sarah Baylis
London, 1987.

VOLUME I

LORD Munster devoted himself entirely to ambition: what has been said of Cinna might be applied to him, *he had a head to contrive, a tongue to persuade, and a hand to execute any mischief.* Weak people are only wicked by halves; and whenever we hear of high and enormous crimes, we may conclude that they proceeded from a power of soul, and a reach of thought, that are altogether unusual.

He stuck at nothing to accomplish his political plans; and his success rendered him still more enterprising: But being at last refused a favor from his Sovereign, he retired disgusted with the court, and in vain sought that happiness in a retreat, which his crimes made it impossible he should ever find. He was so chagrined that everything became intolerable to him; and he continually vented his spleen on those of his friends, whose circumstances rendered them subservient to his caprices. He possessed good health, a large estate, and had fine children, that equalled his most sanguine expectations. In the opinion of the world, therefore, he was *a very happy man*, but in his own, *quite the contrary*. No man can judge of the happiness or infelicity of his neighbour. We only know the external causes of good and evil, which causes are not always proportionable to their effects: those which seem to us small, often occasion a strong sensation; and those which appear to us great, often produce only a faint sensation. The great advantages Lord Munster possessed, as they excited in him only indifference, in reality were inconsiderable in themselves. But the small evil, his having been refused a ribbon by his Sovereign, exciting in him insupportable uneasiness, was in reality a great evil. Lady Munster had been dead many years: Lord

Finlay and Lady Frances were the only surviving children. Engrossed as the earl had been in public affairs, he still paid particular attention to their education. Though a man of the world, he was at the utmost pains in selecting those of distinguished worth, to whom only he committed the care of his children. Lord Finlay had promising parts; but force of mind makes a man capable of great vices or great virtues, but determines him to neither.

Education, discipline, and accidents of life, constitute him either a profound philosopher, or a great knave. The probity and disinterestedness of Mr Burt's principles recommended him to Lord Munster, for a tutor to his son. – He had been brought up to the ministry, with an inclination to it, and entered into it with a fervent desire of being as useful as he could. His education being all his fortune, he subscribed, and took every step the church required, before he was sufficiently acquainted with the doctrines subscribed to; – their foundation in scripture, and the controversies which he afterwards found had been raised, and carried on about them in the christian world: and, after a diligent inquiry, was dissatisfied with some doctrines established in our articles, liturgy, &c. and declined accepting a considerable living in Lord Munster's gift, on which *alone* he depended for his future subsistence, and that of an amiable woman, whom he had espoused upon these expectations.

I heartily wish that all who are disposed for the ministry of the church, were as careful to satisfy themselves about the lawfulness of *conformity*, and that the church of England laid fewer obstructions in the way of those who are both disposed and qualified for advancing the interests of religion and virtue; but dare not engage publicly in her service, for fear of violating the peace of their minds, and wounding their consciences. In such a situation what must a clergyman do? must he preach and maintain doctrines he disapproves of? this would be acting both against his persuasion, and his solemn promise at his ordination. Shall he preach or write against them? this he must not do neither, lest he should be judged guilty of impugning his subscription, and consequently incur the censures of the church. Shall he then be quite silent, and neither preach nor write about them at all? but how will this be consistent, with his other solemn promise, made likewise at his ordination, *to be ready with all faithful diligence, to banish and drive away all erroneous and strange doctrines* – all doctrines which he *is persuaded*, are contrary to God's word? He must therefore necessarily offend, either against the church, or against truth, and his own conscience. A sad alternative! when a man can neither speak, what he thinks to be truth, with *safety*, nor be silent without *offence*. These considerations induced Mr Burt to refuse a proffered establishment – by which conduct, he proved his belief in a *future state*, more firmly than a great many of them appear to do, by their immoderate desires of the good things *in this*: but his faith was founded, not on the fallacious arguments of too many of his brethren; but on that adorable conjunction of unbounded power and goodness, which must certainly someway recompense so many thousand innocent wretches, created to be so miserable here. He possessed that virtue in an eminent degree, which the christians call humility, and which the ancients were ignorant of. – But he had real merit, and could easily be modest, which is almost impossible to those, who have only the affectation of it. With this respectable man was Lord Finlay placed, at five years old, when a considerable settlement was made on him, in compensation for relinquishing other pursuits, with a promise of its beings continued for life. Lord Munster from time to time examined his son, and was highly satisfied with the progress he made; and not a little surprised, to find him no way deficient in those accomplishments, which, though of less consequence in themselves, a late noble author has illustrated as being absolutely necessary, in compleating the character of a fine gentleman. For these Lord Finlay was indebted to Captain Lewis, father-in-law to Mr Burt. This old gentleman was of an antient family, and had retired from the army, disgusted at his situation, having been many years in a very subaltern station.

The condition of many brave and experienced officers is to be lamented, who, after having passed through many various dangers in the service of their country, are subject to the command of boys and striplings. Whilst stations, which should be the reward of martial virtues, can be purchased, it is in vain to hope, that our officers can be animated like those of a neighbouring nation.

Honour alone can support the soldier in a day of battle; without this invigorating principle, humanity will tremble at the sight of slaughter, and every danger will be avoided, which necessity does not impose.

Captain Lewis retained that dignity of sentiment, which no misfortunes could surmount. Our hearts and understandings, are not subject to the vicissitudes of fortune. We may have a noble soul though our circumstances be circumscribed, and a superiority of mind without being of the highest rank. He had been much among the *great world*, in the early part of his life, having been *aide-de-camp* to Lord S———. Upon his daughter's marriage with Mr Burt, he resided entirely with him; and though she died of her first child, he continued with him, and became as fond of lord Finlay as his grand-daughter, who, after her mother's decease, became the object of his tenderest affection.

Thus were Lord Finlay and Miss Burt brought up together; and from the time of her birth never separated until she was nine years old. At that period she was sent to a convent at Paris, and returned, after six years absence, highly accomplished; uniting in herself everything that could charm a heart that was disengaged.

The consequences to Lord Finlay were inevitable, though never suspected. A student of about eighteen, full of the amours of Ovid, and the soft odes in Horace, has a heart very susceptible of love. These sensations were too agreeable to be repulsed; he delivered himself entirely over to his passion, which absorbed every other faculty of his soul. The most perfect affection soon subsisted between these young people: but the dignity of Miss Burt's manners inspired her lover with such respect as rendered him silent on the subject of his passion, as he could not enforce it without his father's sanction.

But there is an intelligence between tender souls, and the most animated expression may be conveyed without the aid of words; and this dumb language is so eloquent, that it is generally understood where the heart is in unison. Friendship, indeed, was only spoke of; but their every look, their every action, bespoke the most ardent love. 'What transports,' (said he, one day to her) 'can friendship bestow! what refined feelings, what delightful sensations, actuate the human soul in such happy moments as these!'

We contemplate each other in silence; but the soul is never more eloquent than under the influence of such a silence. She expresses, in a moment, a train of ideas and sensations, which would be but confounded by utterance.

Miss Burt had a merit the more engaging, from its avoiding notice and parade: a refined genius, enriched with great knowledge and happy expression, united with the most candid sincerity and goodness of heart; these qualities entitled her to the esteem and friendship of every noble mind: and the thick veil, under which her too great modesty concealed her pre-eminence, exalted her in the penetrating eyes of her lover. She scarce ever laid *this veil* aside, except to him, whose approbation rendered her indifferent with respect to the commendations of every one else. He became every day more attached to her: and was so ignorant of the world as to expect his father's approbation of his passion, and that he would be propitious to it.

Thus situated were the lovers, when Lord Munster disgusted with the court retired to the country. He immediately sent for Mr Burt and Lord Finlay: although the distance was only a few miles, it was very grievous for the latter to leave a place where he had access every minute of the day to behold the object of his wishes.

Upon this occasion he was determined to disclose to her the situation of his heart. He threw himself at her feet, in that pathetic disorder of spirits which constitutes the true eloquence of love, and endeavoured to speak, but hesitated at every word. In the mean time she saw and pitied his confusion.

'I can read,' said she, 'my lord,' with an air of frankness, 'the sentiments of your heart: I am not insensible of your passion; but why hath fortune placed us at so great a distance from each other? how delightful it would have been to me, if – But, said she, (stopping short in her discourse) 'let us not flatter ourselves with chimeras. – Let us suppress the emotions of our hearts; it may be dangerous to indulge them.'

'How? dangerous!' replied Lord Finlay, 'why suppress them? do not those emotions constitute our happiness? It is the duty of love to repair the injustice of fortune. How enraptured should I be to make happy the object I love. Prejudice might object to it perhaps: but that shall never enslave my understanding, especially as it must be founded only in pride.'

With these sentiments they parted. It may be easily conceived how impatient Lord Finlay was to see the idol of his heart, but he could not with propriety propose quitting his father, for the first days after his arrival in the country. He at last fell upon the expedient of suggesting, whether, as he was under such obligations to Captain Lewis, it would not be proper to call, and invite him to Munster house. This Lord Munster agreeing to, he and his son called one morning; when Miss Burt entertaining them with a little music, the light-winged god took one of the sharpest arrows from the fair-one's quiver, applied it to his bow, and swift as the forked lightning of Jove, fixed it in the old man's heart. Lord Munster became desperately in love, and determined to make her his wife. It is not at all surprising that a young woman makes an impression on an old man. While we have life we have our passions; age *represses*, but does not *extinguish* them. As in maturer years, the fire lurks under the ashes of prudence; so, if that be wanting, love burns up and blazes fiercely; and is generally inextinguishable, if it takes hold of the dry and worm-eaten wood of old-age. Persons of languid passions (it has been observed) have few partialities; they neither love, nor hate, nor look, nor move, with the energy of a man of sense. People of real genius, and strong passions, have great partialities. The blamelessness of the former should be weighed with their insignificancy; and the faults of the latter balanced with their superiority.

Lord Munster made proposals to Mr Burt that very day, never doubting but that Hymen would soon rekindle his *torch*. – But the same principles determined him respecting his daughter, which had influenced him in his own affairs. He thanked Lord Munster for the honor he intended him, which he should acquaint her of – but that in an affair in which her happiness for life was so immediately concerned, he must forgive his interfering further. When he acquainted her with it; instead of enforcing the acceptance of the honor proposed to her, he was at great pains to precaution her, against many disagreeable consequences of such an unequal alliance, both in age and condition, lest she should be dazzled by wealth or titles, to sacrifice her inclinations!

Miss Burt, with unfeigned concern, was greatly chagrined to hear of Lord Munster's proposals: she, therefore, with great warmth, declared herself totally unfit, for such an exalted station. 'I can neither,' said she, 'adopt the virtues, or the vices of the great: the former are too conspicuous, the other too obscure. A round of peaceable employments, proper to satisfy the mind, and to soothe the heart, is the kind of happiness for which I find myself inclined.'

'With such principles and inclinations, I could not be happy in the great world, where the general way of life is solely calculated, to flatter the senses, and where a superior genius is contemned, or at least only permitted to exhibit itself in lively sallies, or smart repartees.'

Mr Burt informed the earl of his daughter's sentiments. But his lordship's self-love prevailed so far as to render it impossible to conceive that *he could be refused*. He, therefore, made preparations for his nuptials, and sent for his daughter home to be present on that occasion. Lord Munster had taken the same pains on Lady Frances's education, as her brother's. Mrs Norden, a distant relation, had the entire charge of her. She resided in London until Lady Frances was fourteen years old: at that time she accompanied her to Rome, where she had the best masters, and where Santerello improved her taste in music. After remaining three years at Rome, they went to Paris, from which they were just returned at the period above mentioned. Lord Munster was greatly charmed, both with the personal, and acquired perfections of his daughter: and professed himself much indebted to Mrs Norden, for the very great attention she had paid to her.

The day after Lady Frances's arrival, she went to Mr Burt's to pay her respects to her intended mother-in-law.

No servant happening to be in the way to announce her, she walked forwards into a room, the door of which she saw open, with an intention to ring the bell, when she found Miss Burt in her father's library, weeping bitterly: never before had she seen such an air of languid softness, mixed with so much beauty. What an affecting sight! She was going to retire, to save her from that confusion which a sensible heart is apt to feel at having its afflictions perceived by a stranger; but the lovely mourner, observing her, endeavoured to suppress her emotions: but her grief was too violent to be checked; and her tears burst forth the more, for having been an instant subdued. She could only say, 'That she could be no stranger to *who* did her the honour of waiting on her, from the likeness Lady Frances had to her brother.' The thoughts of Lord Finlay then renewed her affliction; and asking pardon for her rudeness, she again shed a torrent of tears. Lady Frances answered, 'That apologies were only due on her part, for breaking in upon her retirement, and witnessing emotions she might have wished to conceal.' After a few general things, she told her the pleasure it gave her of having so near a prospect of being entitled to take an interest in all her concerns; when she would be happy in her friendship. In this Lady Frances was perfectly sincere; for though she had been alarmed at the intended marriage taking place, and although she was of a very shy disposition, yet, at first sight, feeling the greatest partiality for Miss Burt, she echoed her sighs, and her eyes bore testimony of the feelings of her heart. With all the confidence of an ancient friendship, she conjured her to acquaint her with the cause of her sorrows; and took upon her to console, soothe, and comfort her. Miss Burt had only time to express the sense she entertained of her goodness, and to add, her miseries were *too great* to be *alleviated*; when her grand-father entering the room, the conversation turned upon general topics.

Upon Lady Frances's return home, her father gayly enquired, What she thought of his intended bride? She answered, Every thing that was charming; and that she had prepared for her an eternal habitation in the warmest part of her heart: 'There is every thing in her,' added she, 'that can engage the affections, or command the respect, of people of taste and judgment.'

Lord Finlay mean while was under the greatest oppression of spirits. A thousand conflicting passions tortured his (until then) undisturbed bosom. Love and filial piety alternatively took possession of his soul. Each in their turn was rejected. – When sentiments are nearly of equal force, the soul, as if unsettled, and wavering between contrary emotions, knows not which to resolve on; its decrees destroy each other; scarce is it freed from its troubles when it is involved in them anew; this undetermined state does not always terminate to the advantage of the most powerful sentiment.

After a long conflict, the soul wearied out with the efforts it has made, gradually loses its sensibility and force together; and finally yields to the last impression, which thus remains master of the field. After many struggles, Lord Finlay was determined to sacrifice his *inclinations*, or in other words, (what he thought, his life, to his father.)

This pious resolution, no doubt, was strengthened by his supposing Miss Burt had acquiesced to the proposed marriage. His resentment supported his prudence. Such was the situation of Lord Finlay's mind, when Lady Frances received the following letter from Miss Burt.

'Madam,

You found me in tears, and kindly insinuated your desire to mitigate my distress; receive from me all the acknowledgments which can proceed from a full heart, raised from the lowest distress, to a glimmering prospect of avoiding misery, while that superior Power which witnesses your generosity, will *reward it.* Thus, when unhappy, we grasp at the least shadow of relief! we seize upon it with eagerness, and in a moment raise ourselves above our afflictions. When an unhappy drowning wretch is carried away by the current, while intimidated by the steepness of the banks, and the rapidity of the torrent, he looks upon death as inevitable; his sinews relax, his heart fails him, he looks forward to an awful dreaded futurity: but if the least twig presents its friendly assistance, his courage at last revives, he raises his head, he seizes upon it with a hasty avidity, and makes a sudden and violent effort to save himself from destruction. Such is my application to your ladyship. Heaven grant you may avert from me those evils I so much dread! even the horror of involving my respectable parents *in want and misery.* My father's probity has entailed on him poverty; and my grandfather's half-pay is our sole dependance, exclusive of the salary Lord Munster settled on my respectable parent when he undertook to superintend the education of his son; and which he promised to continue for life, in compensation for his giving up *all other pursuits.* I flatter myself, the frowardness of his unhappy daughter will not frustrate his lordship's beneficence, and which he judged his labours entitled him to. May I intreat your ladyship will soften, through the medium of your influence, the refusal of the honor intended me!

An attempt to deceive would wring my soul to torture: Can I then take upon me vows at the altar, incompatible with the feelings of my heart, and the possibility of conforming myself to? forbid it, gratitude, truth, and justice! let me sooner become a martyr to these, as my unfortunate father. In every event of my life, integrity and honor shall influence me. If my refusal is not founded upon the most *advantageous*, yet it is upon the most *worthy* terms: if that of embracing *tranquility* before *profit*, and preferring probity of mind, even attended with the greatest inconveniences, before its opposite, although surrounded with every outward accommodation, be deserving of that epithet. I ask pardon for this intrusion, and have the honor to be

    Your Ladyship's
      Obliged humble servant,
      MARY ANN BURT.'

The little tenderness Lord Munster had ever shewn Lady Frances, the impressions she entertained of the sourness of his disposition, and the severity of his temper; all conspired to fill her with the greatest awe and dread of his displeasure. It may then be easily judged how badly qualified she was for the office enjoined her in the letter. To add to her distress, her valuable friend Mrs Norden was absent, and she dared not conceal the receipt of it until her return, as it was a subject that admitted of no delay.

She accordingly summoned up sufficient courage to take the letter in her hand, and to present herself before her father; when her timidity and confusion were sufficient vouchers of her unwillingness to be an agent in such a disagreeable business. Her apprehensions were considerably increased, when the earl asked her, in a harsh tone, *her business with him?* Being unable to reply, and trembling from head to foot, she gave him the letter – which he eagerly pursued, while he was alternately agitated with indignation, pride, and confusion! He at length broke into a great rage, loading Lady Frances with invectives, for having innocently produced these emotions, adding, that he then discovered the cause of her partiality for Miss Burt: but that if she, or Lord Finlay, ever presumed, from that time forward, to hold any communication with *the Burt family*, he should consider them as aliens *to his!* Where friendship is reversed, and turned to enmity, the *latter* is generally as *extreme*, as the *former* was *fervent*. If we were more regular in *our affections*, we should be more moderate in *our aversions*, and, without consulting our interest, should hate nothing but what is really odious: but we are so unjust, that we judge only of things by their relation to us; we approve of them when agreeable to us, and, by a strange infatuation, do not esteem them as good or bad, but by the satisfaction of disgust they give us: we would have them alter their quality according to our caprices, and cameleon like, assume our colours, and accommodate themselves to our desires. We fain would be the center of the world, and have all creatures join with us in inclination. Lord Munster was not only disappointed in his affections, but piqued in pride, that, after he had by his intrigues led some of the first princes in Europe, and made them subservient to his views, a little obscure girl should render him the laughing-stock of the country. Lady Frances retired, not daring to return him any answer.

Lord Finlay met her, and, alarmed at her appearance, followed her into her apartment, intreating to know the subject of the letters she had received from Miss Burt! She informed him of it, and the disagreeable task she had just executed; when his looks very soon (to one of her penetration) betrayed the situation of his heart. He owned to Lady Frances that his life depended on Miss Burt, their mutual affection, and the violence he had done his inclinations, by the obligations he had imposed on himself to subdue his passion whilst it interfered with his father: but remarked with joy, that he was now relieved from such a painful effort. 'The Almighty,' said he, 'my dear sister,' (for he was in a state of mind which both inclined him to be wise and kind) 'implanted both reason and the passions in human nature, mutually to conduce to mens happiness. But, in order to become a happy creature, man is not blindly to follow the impulses of his passion to the exclusion of reason: nor is he to contradict his natural desires but when they invert the order of nature, and oppose the common good of society, the dictates of right reason, and the manifest design of Providence. – I have done what man could do,' added he; 'I did not interefere when my father was concerned; but I will not relinquish the object of my affections to any other man breathing.' This was Lord Finlay's philosophy, which he strictly adhered to – Tremblingly alive to his interest, Lady Frances told him the risque he would run of his father's displeasure; but the impetuosity of his passion rendered him deaf to her remonstrances; and, regardless of everything but its gratification, he sat down and wrote the following letter to Miss Burt.

'Madam,

The strict injunctions of my father, that all communication should cease between our families, renders it necessary for me to *write*, instead of *waiting* on you in person. Alas, how poor a substitute is the former for the latter! To express my sorrow, or paint my grief, is impossible! Were you to know my distress, you would be sensible of my sufferings, and compassionate my wretchedness! To be debarred from the presence of your respectable parents, to whom I have a thousand obligations, and for whom I feel the greatest respect an tenderest regard, is a very great hardship: but to be prevented from beholding you, is downright tyranny, and forces me to rebel! Could I see Mr Burt, I would intreat him to pardon, what I am mortified to call the injustice of my father, and assure him that nothing shall be wanting, on my part, to soften, and bring him to reason. But I know too well the inflexibility of his virtue, he will not see me contrary to the inhibitions I have received.

Permit me on my knees to intreat from you that favor I dare not request from him! We may meet at — any day before seven in the morning. My life depends on your answer! Let us at least enjoy the soothing pleasure, the melancholy consolation of mingling griefs, and bearing a part in each other's sorrows; satisfaction that even renders despair itself more tolerable! Be persuaded there is nothing, not even my father, that can divert my eye, my heart, or hand, from an opportunity of expressing how much I am, with the greatest respect,

> Your devoted
> > Humble servant,
> > > FINLAY'

After dispatching the above letter, Lord Finlay spent his time, fluctuating every moment between hope and despair, agitated with all the pains of a solicitous suspence; but Miss Burt was too much attached to him not to agree to his proposal, nor did her condescension at all infringe on her delicacy. – She could not suppose that the good qualities so distinguishable in her lover, and which had been so studiously cultivated by *her father*, could be *only* violated to the dishonor of *his daughter*. Lord Finlay's passion was too ardent to submit to prudence, and could not be long concealed: they met often, and remained long together; time is easily forgot in the society of those we love – In Cupid's dial, *hours* are but *minutes*. – Their interviews were discovered.

Captain Lewis being informed of it, jealous of his honor, insisted on Lord Finlay's instantly espousing his grand-daughter; who, loaded with his reproaches, led away by his passion, and the fears of being interdicted from steering her more – forgot every thing but the justification of his honorable intentions.

The indignation with which Lord Munster was seized when informed of this marriage, is easier to be conceived than delineated. He swore he would never see his son more, or contribute to his support!

The passions are more easily excited in the young than in the old; in women, as being of a frame more delicate than in men; in the poor and distressed, than in the rich and fortunate, for prosperity hardens the heart; in the illiterate than in the learned, because more prone to admire; and for the same reason in those who have lived privately, than in men of large experience; but when once fixed, are not so easily eradicated as in the others.

The indiscreet solicitations of a gentleman in the neighbour-hood, served only to exasperate him *the more*. A weak friend, if he will be kind, ought to go no further than wishes: if he either says or does more, it is *dangerous*. Good intentions are indispensable to constitute a good man; but other adjuncts are necessary to form the man who interferes in our behalf. An excellent cause has often suffered through an indifferent advocate; and I once heard of a lawyer retained by his client, to *hold his peace for him*.

In consequence of Lord Munster's implacability, Lord and Lady Finlay were involved in a variety of wretchedness, and most affecting distress; under all which they bore up with becoming fortitude, and never departed from that dignity of behaviour, which innate virtue, and conscious innocence inspire; strengthened by true principles of religion, and a rational trust in providence, tempered with genuine humility, and unfeigned resignation to whatever fate should be alloted them. In every action of their lives they had a view to each other: if they were serious, or cheerful, amused or grieved, still by their sympathy and love, every trifle made a pleasure, and every pleasure was heightened into rapture, by their mutual participation of it. Their hearts exulted with that joy which is built on the strong foundation of undissembled tenderness. Happy it is for mortals, that grief is only an exotic in the human breast – the soil does not naturally afford nutriment for its constant growth. A perfect similarity of sentiment soon produced that mutual happiness which arises from loving another better than one's self: they were no longer anxious for events they could not direct, nor tasted pain from the disappointment of their hopes.

The half-pay of Captain Lewis, was the only ostensible support of his unfortunate family, increased by the birth of several children: but their income had been enlarged, by Mr Burt's literary productions. His greatest enjoyment was in study – pleasures vary with each different age; for God and nature never made any faculty, either in soul or body, but he prepared a suitable object in order to its regular gratification.

The follies of men of a certain age, on this account, have the pre-eminence to all others, a ridiculous dignity, that gives them a right *to be laughed at in the first place*. The phenomenon of feeling amorous pursuits under grey hairs, may as much astonish us, as to see those mountains whose top is covered with snow, and whose bowels abound with flames. Mr Burt had a happy temper, formed on the principles of Christian philosophy. Such was his cheerfulness, that none of the accidents of life could discompose him; such his fortitude, that not even the severest trials could unman him. He had a collected spirit, and on no occasion wanted a resource. He could retire within himself, and hold the world at defiance.

His amiable daughter possessed also these qualities in an eminent degree. Captain Lewis dying, their circumstances were reduced; but Lady Finlay, by her ingenuity supplied the loss they sustained in his half-pay. She had a fine genius for painting, and in that art did wonders. By the sale only of a *Crucifixion*, and an *Arcadia*, she maintained her family for two years. She concealed her name, lest she should irritate Lord Munster more against her; but had too much good sense to be ashamed of employing those talents, bestowed on her by nature for *so natural a purpose*. And the hours that the *indolent* devote *to rest*, and the licentious to *pleasure*, she dedicate to providing bread for her family. Good blood cannot be kept up, without the shambles of the market, so it is no scandal to procure *that* by ingenuity or industry, when the appendages of gentility are so far reduced as not to afford it otherwise.

The picture called Arcadia, is in the possession of the Marquis of P———. In it there is exhibited a view of the most delightful region, with the grandest rural scenery in the world; and a romantic wildness runs through the whole, which gives uncommon beauties to the piece. Her happy fancy, and the prospects in the country (they had retired to Wales for cheapness) supplied her with vales more charming than those of *Juan Fernandez*, with lawns like those of *Tinian*, and finer water-falls than those of *Quibo*. She copied the greatest beauties in nature, and formed the finest imitations. The invention of the whole is extremely pleasing; and has been applauded by all who have seen it, as a master piece in the landscape way.

Lady Finlay's health decreasing she could no longer *exert this talent*; and the miserable situation to which her Lord was reduced, in consequence of his attachment to her, afforded her constant uneasiness. The griping hand of poverty, produced painful fears, and corroding cares, while the anxiety of mind *each* suffered for *the other*, increased their *mutual calamity*.

The death of two fine children at last entirely subdued Lady Finlay's remaining spirits – She died in child-bed, (the infant surviving her a few hours) leaving behind her only two children. It was then Lord Finlay's cup of affliction was filled. He had reason to fear, the deceased, dearest object of his tenderest affections, had perished for want of proper assistance. *Assistance!* their scanty circumstances denied! If previous to this, when he perceived in her any marks of sorrow, it was to him as if all nature had been eclipsed; what must have been his sensations *then?* they were too great for humanity to support! His reason forsook him; and the third day after her decease, he expired in the delirium of madness.

Nothing can give a better sense of the consideration man ought to have of his latter end, than the following lines of Sir Thomas More:

> 'You'd weep, if sure you'd but one month to stay;
> Yet laugh, uncertain of a single day!'

Few are the happy marriages contracted contrary to the consent of parents. – Disobedience to them, like murder, seldom goes unpunished in this life*. Mr Burt wrote Lady Frances Finlay a letter informing her of the melanocholy catastrophe of this unfortunate couple, and beseeching her interest with Lord Munster, in behalf of their helpless progeny.

* See the Fifth Commandment.

'Could tears, Madam,' said he, 'write as legibly as ink, my streaming eyes would be an inexhaustible fund, to assist me to send you the woes of a poor old man, and to pour forth the sorrows of my soul! But *Cicero* could not have *described*, *Apelles* could not have *painted*, nor *Roscius* have *represented*, the heart-rending scenes I have lately witnessed.'

Lord Munster died the day before his daughter received the above letter. He had for some time before lost all sensation. The pleasures or pains of others were to him of so little importance, that he lived as if he had been the only creature himself in the universe. He could not bear to hear of the applause some of his opponents in politics had acquired, and grudged them a reputation he thought only suitable to his own distinguished abilities. Different from that conqueror, of whom it is said he silenced the whole earth, he fancied that the whole world must talk of his disgrace. He could not support it; and a pistol put an end to his wretched existence. A careful observer of events will frequently see, that flagrant vices are punished by some remarkable strokes of wretchedness, and bad dispositions made sensible of the evils they bring on others. Never did any Greek or Roman commit suicide, from too quick a sense of private misfortunes. – Vain glory in the vulgar may be supportable, nay, may be diverting; but in a great man it is *intolerable*: nothing is greater in a man, than to be above even greatness *itself*.

Lady Frances was left by her father the entire possession of the family estate. – She immediately wrote to Mr Burt, desiring he would leave a place which must necessarily revive in him such melancholy ideas, and bring her nephew and niece to Munster house; enclosing him a sum of money to discharge debts, and to defray the expenses of the journey. He instantly complied with her request, and resided with her, though she immediately not only settled on him the annuity he had formerly been promised, but also paid the arrears due on it.

Had Lord and Lady Finlay lived a few weeks longer, Lady Frances would have cheerfully assigned to them the estate bequeathed to her, and which their virtues so justly entitled them to.

It is a strong argument for a state of retribution hereafter, that in this world *virtuous people* are often *very miserable*, and *vicious ones happy*, which is wholly repugnant to the nature of a Being, who appears infinitely wise and good in all his works, unless we may suppose, that such a promiscuous and undistinguishing distribution of good and evil, which was necessary for carrying on the designs of Providence in this life, will be rectified and made amends for in another.

Lady Frances possessed the most attractive beauty, was surrounded with every grace, and blessed with every virtue, that could enslave the affections, and captivate the soul of the most stubborn philosophers. The sound of her voice had an engaging sweetness; and her expressions were well chose, without being affected. – In a word, it was her character and mind that gave charms to her person. Lord Darnley made his addresses to her, in which he had been countenanced by Lord Munster, and every preparation was making for their nuptials, before her father's death.

Lord Darnley was one of the most amiable of men. He gave a grace to every thing he said – a refined and delicate wit enlivened all his discourse, and the vivacity of his imagination discovered itself continually in fresh sallies. But what irresistibly fixed Lord Munster's partiality; was the art with which he disguised his *own wit* and *knowledge* to make *him shine*. He conformed entirely to that pleasing criterion of true humour which Mr Addison gave, – 'That it looks grave itself, while it makes all others laugh.' He had a turn for placing things in a ridiculous point of view, which was highly diverting – but by this he never offended; he formed his ridicule on a circumstance, which the party attacked, was not in his heart unwilling to grant him; that he was guilty of an excess in something which in itself was laudable*. He very well understood what he chose to be, what was his predominant passion, and knew he need not fear his anger, for declaring he was a little *too much the thing*.

Nice raillery is a decent mixture of praise and reproach; it touches slightly upon little failings, only to dwell the more upon great qualities. I believe what renders courtiers pleasing, is the attention they pay to the self-love of others. I shall only add, that the politeness of Lord Darnley's manners would not suffer him to omit any of those engaging attentions which are so capable of

---

* Pliny recommends ridicule as an admirable weapon against vice. It is surely better here employed, than as Shaftesbury recommends it, for the test of truth.

pleasing; and as he was deeply in love with Lady Frances, he inspired her with mutual sentiments. How then must it surprise the world to find, that upon her sudden acquisition of wealth, the marriage did not take place! The philosopher, experienced in the vicissitudes of human events, views such sudden dissolutions of the most intimate connections without surprise or amazement. In regard to the moral and political world, it is not always great and adequate causes that produce strange and surprising events; on the contrary, they often are the result of things seemingly small, and utterly disproportionate to their effects. The same constant fluctuation that attends the seasons, and all the appendages of the globe we inhabit, affects the heart of man, making it a prey, by turns, to different passions. The well-regulated mind alone, can boast of any degree of consistency, and *that* too often late in life, the product of long experience, and unnumbered cares. It was in vain Lord Darnley declared the disinterestedness of his passion, and intreated Lady Frances to settle the property of the family out of his power, previous to her marriage.

She remained unmoved; only assured him, that nothing but what she apprehended was her first duty, could alienate her from him, and that she never would dispose of herself to any *other*: but advised him to marry. She applied herself entirely to the care of her family, and to the improvement of that property invested in her person.

Living entirely in the country, she sought, in the beauty of nature, in science, and the love of order, that satisfaction, which in the world (where people are the *slaves of apology, and the dupes of caprice*) is eagerly pursued, but *never found*. It is principally on this account, that people in general are so often declaiming against human life. She considered society is manifestly maintained by a circulation of kindness: we are all of us, in some way or other, wanting assistance, and in like manner qualified to give it. None are in a state of independency on their fellow-creatures. The most slenderly endowed are not a mere burthen on the community; even they can contribute their share to the common good. We learn what are justly our mutual claims, from this mutual dependency; that on its account, as well as for other reasons, our life is not to pass in a round of pleasure of idleness, or according to the suggestions of mere fancy, or in sordid or selfish pursuits. Can there be any thing more evidently our duty than that we should return the kindness we receive; than that, if many are employed in promoting our interest, we should be as intent in advancing theirs? All men are by nature equal: their common passions and affections, their common infirmities, their common wants, give such constant remembrances of this equality, even to those who are most disposed to forget it, that they cannot, with all their endeavours, render themselves unmindful of it. They cannot become *insensible*, how unwilling soever they may be to *consider*, that their debt is as much their demands, as they owe to others as much as they reasonably can expect from them. It is not to be supposed that Providence would have made such distinctions among men, such unequal distributions, but that they might endear themselves to one another by mutual helps and obligations. Gratitude is the surest bond of love, friendship, and society.

The various conditions of human life seem so admirably adapted to the several dispositions of individuals, that if our happiness in this life were intended, the unequal distribution of the gifts of fortune affords the most plausible means to effect it. Through nature, indeed, love is centered at home, and not improperly, though the most amiable and God-like is the most diverged. But as the principle regards of human love, are, for the much greater part, over selfish and contracted, the divine goodness has so directed its operations, as to render them necessary, and very often unintentionally productive of common social good. I have often observed, that people favoured by fortune seldom feel for the pain of the mind, even though they themselves are the authors of it; their pity alone is excited by certain disgraces, certain exterior evils, such as sickness and poverty. This was by no means the case with Lady Frances, who interested herself in the distresses of the soul, with a goodness equally noble and judicious, and offered to the unhappy, all those labouring under any species of innocent distress, consolation and relief.

Her education taught her, that *virtue* and *abilities* can only procure us real happiness, and that nothing but *doing good*, in that sphere of life in which we are placed, can afford the true felicity to a noble soul. Upon her father's death she found herself possessed of an estate of twenty thousand pounds a year, and three hundred thousand pounds in mortgages. The house and pleasure grounds were in great disrepair, from the late Earl's constant residence in London and the *environs*. Lady Frances sent for Mr Brown, who found great *capabilities* in the situation: under his direction it is now one of the finest places in England. She acquainted him of her intention of building a number of houses for the reception of artificers, and the introduction of certain manufactures. He fixed upon a beautiful situation, at the side of a navigable river. Mr Adams approved very much of the plan Lady Frances submitted to his inspection – he perfected and improved it. It consisted of one hundred houses; and a *tribuna** in the center. Upon the solid foundation of the Doric, the Ionic, and Corinthian orders rise gradually with all their beauty, proportion, and ornaments.

The fabric seizes the most incurious eye. No modern building is comparable to it for the outward decorations; and for the disposition within, it has been formed from whatever ancient and modern times afford most adapted and suitable to the purpose of the structure, not excluding decorations, which are distributed with equal taste and economy. The sciences and arts are assembled together in this fine building, and connected (if I may be allowed the expression) by a large and well chosen library in all faculties: Here is whatever the lower people's interest, or the man of taste's curiosity can desire. The first object that presents itself to the eye, on entering into this noble hall, which is no less spacious than splendid, is the statue of the founder, inviting the lovers of literature to make use of the helps which she has provided for them. This statue is of white marble, as large as life, and entirely worthy of Mr More, the artist; who has improved the exact likeness with an air of grandeur and benevolence, dignity and affability.

And what is a very well chosen ornament for such a place, there is a representation of nine of the most eminent libraries – the Babylonian, Athenian, Alexandrian, Palatine, etc. – with short inscriptions giving an account of each. And to set in view, the origin and first advance of learning in several countries – there are painted on large pilasters ranged along the middle of the library, those persons who were reputed to have been the inventor of letters in several languages. Adam, Abraham, Moses, Mercurius,

---

* *Tribuna*, a term applied to a building quite round, or such as consists of many sides and angles, as the famous room within the great Duke's gallery at Florence: sometimes it is applied for a building, whose area or plan is semicircular, as the section of a cupola.

Ægyptius, Hercules, Cadmus, Cecrops, Pythagoras, and several others, with the letters which each of these are said to have invented written under their pictures.

This library is open at stated times, (like that of the Vatican, and the French king's) with every proper accommodation to all strangers. This was greatly wanted in this kingdom. London, after so many ages, remains without any considerable public library. The best is the Royal Society's: but even that is inconsiderable; neither is it open to the public; nor are the necessary conveniences afforded strangers for reading or transcribing. The British Museum is rich in manuscripts, the Harleian Collection, the Cottonian Library, the collection of Charles I. and many others, especially on our own history; but it is wretchedly poor in printed books: and it is not sufficiently accessible to the public; their revenue not being sufficient to enable them to pay a proper number of attendants.*

An ingenious Persian lately in England, gave an account of many thousand Arabian manuscripts, totally unknown to the gentlemen of the university of Oxford. It is to be wished these were procured. The Orientals and Hebrews were the parents of knowledge, and the Greeks no more than their scholars: how gross were their notions of prudence and *virtue*, till Orpheus, and the travelled philosophers taught them better! The institutions of modern nations are not to be compared to those of the ancients, as almost all these had the advantage of being founded by philosophers. Athens and Sparta were the two first formed states of Greece. Solon and Lycurgus, who had seen the success of the plan conducted by Minos in Crete, and who partly copied after that wise prince, erected these two celebrated republics. The sagacious system of Egypt served as a model to all the east.

The astronomical observatory is furnished with the best instruments; anatomy has an amphitheatre, and a spacious room filled with a compleat set of anatomical pieces in wax.

Painting and sculpture, besides a most convenient apartment for the study and practice of these arts, have two large rooms full of models of the most valuable remains of antiquity, taken from the originals.

* The reason polite literature is more cultivated in Paris than London, is on account of the university libraries, and academies of the former.

The pupils of architecture have a hall, crowded with designs and models of the finest pieces, ancient and modern – and there are contiguous apartments where all the liberal sciences are read and taught, as logic, physic, ethics, metaphysics, astronomy, geography, geometry, etc.

These assemblage of studies in every branch is further enriched with curious museums of antiques, and natural history. All these advantages are heightened by the lectures of able professors in every art and every science.

This academy receives two hundred scholars, affords them a liberal support, and leads them through a perfect course of education; from the first elements of letters, through the whole circle of the sciences; from the lowest class of grammatical learning, to the highest degrees in the several faculties. It properly and naturally consists of two parts, rightly forming two estabishments, the one subordinate to the other. The design of the one was to lay the foundation of science; that of other, to raise and compleat the superstructure: the former was to supply the latter with proper subjects; and the latter was to improve the advantages received in the former.

The young gentlemen in the neighbourhood are permitted to receive instructions from the several professors – and a day is set apart, when they examine young people, in order to discover wherein their genius conflicts, and to what kind of studies or employments they naturally are suited. Every man finds in himself a particular bent and disposition to some particular character; and his struggling against it is the fruitless and endless labour of Sisyphus. Let him follow and cultivate *that* vocation, he will succeed in it, and be considerable in one way at least; whereas, if he departs from it, he will at best be *inconsiderable*, probably *ridiculous*. Cicero said, that masters should consider the nature of their scholars, least they should act like unskilful husbandmen, who would sow wheat in a soil, that was only proper for oats. Might it not prove an useful institution if public societies were erected on this plan? By this means most subjects might become beneficial to the public; and not only the arts be brought to perfection, but all the posts of government be well supplied: whereas, we now daily hear complaints of the want of proper persons to direct affairs, whilst the youth are condemned to studies, and matriculated into certain arts or employments before they arrive at years of discretion.

Some parents on the birth of a son determine what profession he is to be of. The father sometimes designs his son for a judge, because his grand-father was one*, which may be as absurd as to design a *weakly child* for a *running footman*, or a *purblind boy* for a *painter*. Sometimes a young man is to be a colonel because he is tall, or an alderman because he has a large belly.

When any remarkable genius displayed itself in any of the young men, their talents have cultivated for that art of science. The master for oratory was recommended by Mr Sheridan, who says that the art of oratory may be taught upon as certain principles, and with as good a prospect of success, as it ever was by the rhetoricians of Greece or Rome, or as the arts of music, painting, etc. are taught by their several professors. He formed himself on Quintilian's institutes of eloquence, who particularly recommends *chironomy*, or gracefulness of action, which took rise in the age of heroism, was practised by the greatest men in Greece, was approved of by Socrates, ranked by Plato amongst the civil virtues, and recommended by Chrysippus in his treatise upon the education of youth. Quintilian had the acquisition of an hundred years after Cicero's death, to improve his knowledge — he had greater opportunities than Cicero ever had to study 'that intellectual relation, that secret charm, in the liberal professions, which, connecting one to the other, combines them all.'

One angle of the *tribuna* is entirely dedicated to the education of women. Twenty young ladies are admitted, and there are funds for their perpetual maintenance, as that of the two hundred scholars. In the selection of these young gentlewomen, she always gives the preference to those who labour under any imperfection of body – endeavouring, by increasing their resources *within themselves*, to compensate for their *outward defects*. When it is found that any of these ladies have a taste for any manual or mental art, they cultivate it, and assist them in the pleasantest means, and by various little attentions confirm these inclinations with all the spirit of pursuit requisite to preserve minds (in general) from that state of languidness and inactivity, whereby life is rendered irksome to

---

* The Chinese are said to adapt an admirable piece of policy; the son is always of the father's trade, which makes them admirable artisians. May not this be the cause of the small progress the arts have made in that part of the world, and of the dull uniformity and want of taste that distinguishes all their works?

those who have never found it unfortunate. In this establishment she entirely runs counter to that of Madame de Maintenon's at Saint Cyr; where the young women, who should have been instructed in rural labours, and economy in the duties of a family, in the employments of *Solomon's virtuous women*, by their education, were only fit to be addressed by men who were rich enough to require in a wife nothing *but virtue*. This is also the foible of too many parents, who all expect their daughters are to fill exalted stations in life, and by educating them with that view, disqualify them for their after lot.

As divines say that some people take more pains to be damned than it would cost them to be saved, so many people employ more thought, memory, and application, to be fools, than would serve to make them wise and useful members of society. The ancients esteemed it an honor to understand the making of every thing necessary for life one's self, without any dependence on others; and it is that which Homer most commonly calls *wisdom* and *knowledge*. He describes old Eumæus making his own shoes, and says, he had built some fine stalls for the cattle he bred. Ulysses himself built his own house, and set up his bed with great art, the structure of which served to make him known to Penelope again. When he left Calypso, it was he alone that built and rigged the ship. – From all which we see the spirit of these ancient times.

These young ladies are not instructed to declaim with grace, or sing with taste; but if they are less amusing, they are infinitely more useful and interesting companions to those they afterwards associate with, whether in the character of wives or friends. Several of them have married very well in the neighbourhood. There is no sentiment more cold, or of shorter continuance, than admiration. We grow weary of a set of features, though ever so beautiful. Between folly, and a homely person, there is this difference; the latter is constantly the same, at least with imperceptible alteration, whilst folly is ever putting on some new appearance, and giving, by that means, fresh pain and disgust. However true this may be, I believe it would require some rhetoric to convince a young man not to prefer the folly that accompanies beauty, to wisdom and deformity. Though Sir Francis Bacon assures us in his natural philosophy, that our taste is never better pleased than with those things which at first created a disgust in us. He gives particular instances of porter, olives, and other things, which the palate seldom approves of at first; but when it has once got a relish of them, generally retains it for life.

The streets, which were built on each side of the *Tribuna*, were uniform, and the houses ornamented with emblematical figures of the different trades intended for the possessors. She permitted them to live rent-free for the two first years, and admitted none but such who excelled in their art. This was certainly very political – By encouraging them in this manner, it enabled them at first to work, and sell their manufactures at a moderate rate; which insured them the business of the neighbouring counties that would otherwise have sent at a greater distance, for what could be equally produced at home.*

The size of the houses decreases gradually from the centre of every street. As Lady Frances spared no expense in the execution, Mr Adams directed it with the greatest taste and propriety. The smallest houses are, indeed, exteriorly, the handsomest, on account of their twisted columns; yet, as they convey an idea of weakness, they always displease when they are made use of as supports to heavy buildings. The different orders succeed each other, from the Corinthian to the Tuscan, according to the size of the houses. Mr Hogarth observes on this head, that the bulks and proportions of objects are governed by fitness and propriety; that it is this which has established the size and proportion of chairs, tables, and all sorts of utensils and furniture; has fixed the dimensions of pillars, arches, etc. for the support of great weights; and so regulated all the orders in architecture.

In the course of ten years Lady Frances brought all the above plans to perfection; which she the more easily effected from Mr Burt's having maintained a correspondence with the *literati* in most parts of the world. And as the encouragement given was great, it is not surprising that her academy became a seat of the muses, and a place to which many resorted for the solution of literary doubts.

If their ears were enchanted by harmony, their eyes were equally ravished by the beauties of painting and sculpture. In this charming mansion is blended the improvement of the arts, with

* The enormous taxes the Spaniards lay on manufactures are the ruin of trade, which would otherwise flourish; and the people are reduced, by that misconduct in their rulers, to purchase from their enemies things they themselves could produce, if the artificers met with proper encouragement.

that of philosophy: an exquisite assemblage of all the sweets of life. Architecture, statuary, painting, and music, find in her a patroness. Refinement of taste in a nation, is always accompanied with refinement of manners. People accustomed to behold order and elegance in public buildings, and public gardens, acquire urbanity in private. The Italians, on the revival of the liberal arts and sciences, gave them the name of *virtù*; from this was derived the term of *virtuoso*, which has been accepted throughout Europe. Should not this appellation intimate, to those who assume it to themselves, that the study of what is beautiful, in nature or art, ought to render them more virtuous than other men. Exclusive of the above buildings, there are others finely adapted to their different purposes, at the same time calculated to ornament the grounds. There are manufactories of different kinds; and silks wrought by hydraulic machines, which renders the workmanship more easy and expeditious. Lady Frances procured artificers from Tuscany for a porcelaine manufacture, which has continued with them from the ancient Etruscans. She has also established a manufacture of earthen ware, procuring models of Etruscan vases in Terra Cotta, made after those in the Vatican library. These are used even in the most common vessels. She also took some pains in regulating the dress of the young women. A country girl returning from the spring with a pitcher of water on her head, perfectly resembles those figures which the most exquisite antiques represent in the same attitude. The great share *variety* has in producing beauty, may be seen in the ornamental part of nature; the shapes and colours of plants, flowers, leaves; the painting in butterflies wings, shells, etc. which seem of little other intended use, than that of entertaining the eye with the pleasure of variety: in this all the senses delight and are equally averse to sameness – The ear is as much offended with one continued note, as the eye is with being fixed to a point, or to the view of a dead wall.

Every building is rendered ornamental to the grounds. There is a botanical garden, which is filled with plants and flowers, which have been presented to Linnæus, from whom she received them, from every part of the globe. One of his pupils resided here, in an elegant habitation, in which there is a rotunda where lectures on botany are given: this fine room is surrounded with exotic plants. Mr Burt entirely concurred with Linnæus, in wishing, that gentlemen designed for theological studies were directed to apply as much time to the study of physics as they spent in metaphysics and logic, which he judges neither so indispensably necessary, nor useful as the former.

Lady Frances also erected an hospital for the reception of two hundred incurables; a thing much wanted in this kingdom, without paying any regard to their country, religion, or disease, requiring no security in case of death. The practice of most of the public hospitals in this country is widely different, the restrictions of admission being such as frequently deprive many from receiving the benefit first intended by the founder. But she had a fund of charity of another stamp, which gave her infinitely more pleasure, as it was free from the ostentation of those acts of public bounty. These were private donations to those whose circumstances were not yet so bad as to oblige them to beg publicly. If an industrious tradesman had a numerous family, little business, or a small stock, she found means to supply his wants, or put him in a way of carrying on his business to greater advantage, in such a manner, as that sometimes he himself did not know the source of his relief; at most, none but the party succoured, and Mr Burt, knew any thing of the matter, for this worthy man was her secret almoner, and searched out for the secret necessities of modest and industrious poor. She had the happiness arising from the consciousness of having maintained numerous families in decent plenty, who, without her well-timed and secret bounty, must have been a charge to the parish. But she was a great enemy to poor-rates, judging with Davenant, that they will be the bane of our manufactures.

Lady Frances was far from being alarmed at the great expenses of her undertakings. She thought her large fortune, and her nephew's long minority, as it put it in her power, could not be better employed than in works of national magnificence. The power and wealth of ancient Greece were most seen and admired in the splendor of the temples, and other sublime structures of Pericles. He boasted, that every art would be exerted, every hand employed, every citizen in the pay of the state, and the city, not only beautified, but maintained by itself. The sums Lady Frances expended in bringing these plans to perfection, diffused riches and plenty among the people, and has already doubled the estate. She has a fine collection of pictures. – The only way to raise a genius for painting, is to give encouragement: historical painters get so little by their profession, that we have very few. This Lady Frances made her particular object, to afford our youth ready access to good pictures: till these be multiplied in Great Britain, we shall never have the reputation of producing a good painter. If we expect to rival the Italian, the Flemish, or even the French school, our artists must have before their eyes the finished works of the greatest masters. It is a pity, that when an ingenious gentleman* last winter submitted to the parliament, as worthy of their attention, some considerations that might tend to the encouragement of useful knowledge, and the advancement in this kingdom of the arts and sciences, he did not with his usual intelligence, represent the bad consequences of the duty laid on pictures imported into Great Britain: Were the bad effects of this represented to our legislature, it is impossible but it must be amended. This gentleman took notice in his speech, that a remarkable opportunity of improving the national taste in *painting*, which was lately lost, he hoped would now be recovered. The incomparable Sir Joshua Reynolds, and some other great painters, who do honor to our country, generously offered to adorn the cathedral of St Paul's (a glorious monument of the magnificence of our ancestors) with some of their most valuable works: but the proposition was rejected by the late Bishop of London**, though he flatters himself it will be renewed, and accepted by the gentleman at present in that fee†, who is not only a man of *solid piety*, but of the *soundest learning*, and of *equisite classical taste*. The great art of human life is not to eradicate the passions, but to adopt the proper objects of them: if mankind cannot think so abstractedly as a pure effort of unmixed reason implies, I presume it follows, that some degree of passion is warrantable in devotion. While we are in our present imperfect and embodied state, it will be found necessary to call in *externals* to our aid, for the proper discharge of religious worship. Even among those who in their private devotions are most sincere, external acts and ceremonies, when properly conducted, become real assistances; because the connection

*Mr Wilkes, in the motion to refer to the consideration of the committee of supply the petition of the trustees of the *British Museum*.

** Dr Richard Terrick.

† Dr Robert Lowth.

between the body and soul, between the senses and the imagination, between the passions and the reason of mankind, is so strong and mutual, that they uniformly act and re-act upon one another, and mutually raise the soul to new and higher degrees of fervor.

This was so much Lady Frances's opinion, that she had some fine pieces of painting in her chapel, which is also a very fine new building; the architecture and paintings do honor to the artists – She made it a rule to be constant in her attendance at church. Public acknowledgments of the goodness of God, and application for his blessings, contribute to give a whole community suitable apprehensions of him: and these, if it was her duty to entertain, it was equally her duty to propagate; both as the regard she paid the divine excellencies was expressed, and as the same advantage that she received from such apprehensions, was received by all whom they affected in the same manner.

She had not the smallest degree of superstition, having too much good sense to imagine the Deity can be persuaded to recede from the settled laws of the universe, and the immutability of his nature. But she knows the perfections of God are a ground and sufficient reason for prayer, and that it is both an act and a means of virtue.* She had a mind free from prejudice, adorned with knowledge, and filled with the best principles; a noble firmness in showing these principles, and in maintaining them; in short, every talent joined to the most amiable modesty. She was advised to call her elegant village by the name of *Athens*; but this she declined, naming it *Munster Village*: but she justly thought it deserved it; with this difference, that the inhabitants are too well informed to give into such gross superstitions, and so easily suffer themselves to be imposed upon by astrologers, divines, soothsayers, and many other sorts of conjurers, as the Grecians did.

They excelled in arts; their laws were wise; they had brought everything to perfection that makes life easy and agreeable: but they took little pains in the speculative sciences, geometry,

---

* We may quote from the Zendavsta, a wise and benevolent maxim, which compensates for many an absurdity. He who sows the ground with care and diligence, acquires a greater flock of religious merit than he could gain by the repetition of ten thousand prayers.

Zoraster's Institutes.

astronomy, and physics. The anatomy of plants and animals, the knowledge of minerals and meteors, the shape of the earth, the course of the stars, and the whole system of the world, were still mysteries to them.

The Chaldeans and Egyptians, who knew something of them, kept it a great secret and never spoke of them but in riddles; so that until Alexander's time, and the reign of the Macedonians, they had made no great progress in such learning as might cure them of superstition. An immoderate love of the study of astrology, was a weakness which characterized also the fifteenth century. In the age of Lewis XIV, the court was infatuated with the notion of judicial astrology: many of the princes, through a superstitious pride, supposed that nature, to distinguish them, had writ their destiny in the stars. Victor Amadeus, Duke of Savoy, father to the Duchess of Burgundy, had an astrologer always with him, even after his abdication. The same weakness which gave credit to the absurd chimera, judicial astrology, also occasioned the belief of sorcery and witchcraft; courts of justice composed of magistrates, who ought to have had more sense than the vulgar, were employed in trying persons accused of witchcraft. – Latest prosterity must hear with astonishment that the Madame d'Ancre was burnt at the *Grève* as a sorceress. This unfortunate woman, when questioned by counsellor Courtin concerning the kind of sorcery she had used to influence the will of Mary de Medecis, having answered, *She had used that power only which great souls always have over weak minds*; this sensible reply served only to precipitate the decree of her death*.

It must be confessed there is a strong propensity in man's nature, to assign every thing uncommon to supernatural means. But though I am very apt to believe there is greater credulity in most minds, than will be candidly acknowledged, yet the degree of it must be in proportion to people's ignorance and want of information. Thus the famous doctors of the faculty at Paris, when John Faustus brought the first printed books that had then been seen in the world, or at least seen there, and sold them for manuscripts, were surprised at the performance, and questioned Faustus about it; but he affirming they were manuscripts, and that he kept a great many clerks employed to write them, they were

* See Voltaire's Hist. of the age of Lewis XIV.

satisfied. Looking further, however, into the work, and observing such an exact uniformity throughout the whole, that if there was a blot in one, it was the same in all, etc. etc. etc. their doubts were revived. The learned divines not being able to comprehend the thing, (and that was always sufficient) concluded it must be the *devil*; that it was done by magic and witchcraft; and that, in short, poor Faustus (who was indeed nothing but a mere printer) dealt with the *devil*.

They accordingly took him up for a *magician* and a *conjurer*, and one that worked by the *Black Art*, that is to say, by the help of the devil – and threatened to hang him; commencing a process against him in their criminal courts; when the fear of the gallows induced Faustus to *discover the secret* – that he had been a compositor to Koster of Harlem, the first inventor of printing.

Gardening made a much slower progress among the ancients, than architecture. The palace of Alcinous, in the seventh book of the Odyssey, is grand and highly ornamented; but his garden is no better than what we call a kitchen garden. This also Lady Frances excelled in. She had also a receptacle for all sorts of animals to retire to in their old age. It was of old the custom to bury the favourite dog near the master. To use those of the brute creation who toil for our pleasure, or labour for our profit, with hard and ungenerous treatment, is a species of inhumanity which all men allow to be derogatory from virtue. The authors of wanton cruelty towards the dumb creation, are justly execrated for their brutality. It is a crime which I believe many commit, without either considering the misery *it produces*, or the guilt *it incurs*: and many more, who in fits of causeless or capricious displeasure intend to inflict the misery, have yet no sense that they incur guilt. Lady Frances makes use of buffaloes to draw her ploughs. These animals are far stronger than oxen, and eat less. Why have we not them in this country, and dromedaries and camels?

She cultivates India corn, which grows with vast reeds, which is of great use; and has attempted the culture of rice, and some other things upon boggy ground, with tolerable success. As our cork used to come from France, and now grows in Italy, she has tried it here, where it thrives amazingly; it resembles the evergreen oak, and bears acorns. When you strip other trees of their bark, they die; but this grows stronger, and produces a new coat. She leaves nothing unattempted which has a chance of becoming useful. She also procured sheep from Norway, which are peculiar from having four horns, and being spotted like deer, with a coat of substance betwixt the hair and wool, which is admirable for many uses.

Edward IV has been greatly censured, as taking a very impolitic and injurious measure in making a present to the King of Spain of some Cotswold sheep; the breed of which has been very detrimental to the English woollen manufacture, which has been a national branch of trade ever since. The celebrated Buffon affirms, that our sheep are very far removed from their natural state; from which it has been the usual course of things to decline.

Lady Frances cultivates silk-worms. The ancient Romans for a long time never dreamed that silk could be produced in their country; and the first silk ever seen in Greece, was after the conquest of Persia by Alexander the Great. From thence it was imported into Italy, but was sold at the rate of an equal weight of gold.*

The Persians being the only people of whom it was to be had, would not permit a single egg or worm to be carried out of their country. Hence the ancient Greeks and Romans were so little acquainted with the nature of silk, that they imagined it grew like a vegetable. Holosericum, or a stuff made of silk only, was worn by none but ladies of the first rank.** But men of the greatest quality, and even princes, were contented with subsericum, or a stuff made of half silk; to that Heliogabulus is remarked for being the first who wore holosericum†. In the reign of the emperor Justinian, a trial was made for bringing silk-worms alive to Constantinople, but without success; however, two monks who had been employed in the affair, repeated the trial with silk-worms eggs.‡ The experiment succeeded so well, that to this Constantinopolitan colony, all the silk-worms, and silk manufactures in Europe owe their existence and origin. Till the middle of the twelfth century, all the silken stuffs at Rome and other parts of Europe were of Grecian manufacture. But Roger I. King of Sicily, about the year 1138, invading Greece with a fleet of vessels with two or three benches of oars, called Galeæ or Sagittæ (from whence are

---

* Vid. Vopiscus in Aureliano.
** Tacitus Annal. II. Flav. Vopiscus in vita Taciti Imperat.
† Ælius Lampridius in vita Heliogabali. Primus Romanorum holoserica veste usus fertur, cum jam subserica in usu essent.
‡ Procop. de bello Goth. p. 345.

derived the words galley and saique) and sacking and plundering Corinth, Thebes, and Athens, brought away to Palermo, among other prisoners, a great number of silk weavers to instruct his subjects in that art. From them, as Otto Trisingensis de gestis Frederici, lib. I. cap. 23. informs us, the Italians soon learnt the method of manufacturing silk.

Lady Frances did not restrain farmers, or the sons of farmers from shooting, as none are better entitled to game than those whose property is the support of it.

'See that assemblage of the sons of wealth,
Whose pity and humanity extend
To dumb creation! with what costly care
They study to preserve the brutal race
From *vulgar* persecution! Truly great
Were such benevolence, could their design
Deserve so laudable a name! – Alas! What are they but
monopolists in blood,
That to themselves endeavour to preserve
Inviolate the cruel privilege
Of slaughter and destruction? What is this
But petty tyranny, th' ambitious child
Of luxury and pride? If Heaven indulge
A right to kill, each free-born Briton sure
May claim his portion of the carnage. All
O'er nature's commoners, by nature's law,
Plead equal privilege: what then supports
This usurpation in the wealthier tribe;
The *qualifying* acres? no, proud man,
Possessions give not thee superior claim
To that, which equally pertains to all –
Whose property you timid hare, which feeds
In thy inclosure? thine? denied – allow'd,
Yet if the fearful animal be thine,
Because the innocently crops *to-day*
The herbage of thy freehold, whose will be
The claim *to-morrow*, when thy neighbour's soil
Affords her pasturage? Assuming man!
How is the hardy Briton's spirit tam'd
By thy oppressive pride! – when danger comes

Who shall defend thy property? thyself?
No; that poor Briton, whom thou hast undone
By prosecutions — will he not retort,
"What's liberty to me? 'tis lost! 'tis gone!
"If I must be oppress'd, it matters not
"Who are th' oppressors. Shall I hazard life
"For those imperious lordlings, who denied
"That privilege, which Heaven and nature
      meant
"For food, or sport, or exercise to all?"'
                                        British Philippic.

Mr Burt devoted his time much to his grand-children, though
he was far from wishing to obtrude too much knowledge on their
tender years, as the mind may be overstrained by too intense
application, in the same way as the body may be weakened by too
much exercise before it arrives at its full strength.

Quintilian compares the understanding of children to vessels
into which no liquor can be poured but drop by drop. But there is
a certain season, when our minds may be enlarged — when a great
stock of useful truths may be acquired – when our passions will
readily submit to the government of reason – when right principles
may be so fixed in us, as to influence every important action of our
future lives. If at that period it is neglected, error or ignorance are,
according to the ordinary course of things, entailed upon us. Our
passions gain a strength that we afterwards vainly oppose ——
wrong inclinations become to confirmed in us, that they defeat all
our endeavours to correct them. A superior capacity, an ardent
thirst for knowledge, and the finest dispositions, soon discovered
themselves in Lord Munster; particularly a singular warmth of
affection, and disinterestedness of temper. And although experience evinces, that memory, understanding, and fancy, are seldom
united in one person, yet he is one of those transcendant geniuses,
who is blessed with all three. Mr Burt treated him always with that
distant condescension, which, though it encourages to freedom,
commands at the same time respect. He appeared in different
characters to him, that he might find something new and agreeable
in his conversation.

Montaigne says; 'there is nothing like alluring the passions and

affections; otherwise we only make asses loaded with books.'
Exquisite is the fruit produced by a right temperature of the
different qualities, and mixture of the world and philosophy,
business and pleasure, dignity and politeness. The Romans
termed it *Urbanitas*, the Greeks *Atticism*.

At the age of sixteen years the Earl of Munster having received
every advantage education could bestow on him, fully answered
the most sanguine expectations his aunt had formed of him. She
then insinuated to him his dependent situation – her own
intentions of marrying, the great expenses she had been at in the
various improvements she had made on the estate, which rendered it necessary for him to apply himself to business, as it
would disable her from doing so much for him as she would
have inclined: that as she had bestowed on him every advantage
of education, the alternative before him was that of *application*
on his part, or the utmost severity of *censure* on that of the
world.

Lady Frances adopted this plan with Lord Munster to keep him
ignorant of her intentions in his favor, that she might not obstruct
his exerting all his physical and moral strength in acquiring that
knowledge and virtue he at present so eminently possesses.
Though a man of rank born to a large fortune may have fine
natural parts, yet it takes a great deal to make him a *great man*. His
splendid titles and large estate, are in some degree a bar to those
acquirements, as he rests secure in his rank and independent
fortune. How would the number of the nobility be reduced, were
only those allowed to assume that title who could make good their
claim to it by the distinguished endowments which raised the
founder of the family? A man of rank who is a jockey at
Newmarket rises no higher in my estimation than the lowest
mechanic. Men of literature are the only nobility known in China:
In other countries the laws inflict punishment *on criminal actions*:
there, they do more; *they reward virtue*. If the fame of a generous
action is spread in a province, the mandarin is obliged to acquaint
the emperor, who presently sends a badge of honor to the person
who has so well deserved it. Be their birth ever so low, they
become mandarins of the highest rank, in proportion to the extent
of their worth or learning. On the other hand, be their birth ever
so exalted, they quickly sink into poverty and obscurity if they

neglect there studies which raised their fathers*†

The care, attention, and labour incumbent on men for their support, invigorate both the soul and the body, and they are the natural causes of health and sagacity. Virtue itself would be indolent if she had no passions to conquer and regulate. It is every way our advantage that we have no such slothful paradise as the poets feigned in the golden age: and the alledged blemishes in nature, are either the unavoidable accompanyments or consequences of a structure, and of laws subservient to advantages, which quite over-balance these inconveniences, or sometimes the direct and natural means of obtaining those advantages. The situation of the King of Sardinia, environed on all sides with powerful monarchs, obliges him to act with the greatest circumspection; which circumstance seems to have formed the character of that house. – As Lady Frances was desirous of her nephew's understanding commerce, she proposed his becoming a merchant:— with great modesty, and deference for her opinion, he submitted to her, whether the confined maxims of a trader were not destructive of the social virtues; if they did not tend to destroy those refined feelings of the soul that distinguish man from man?‡ She answered, 'What situation is like that of a man, who with one stroke of a pen makes himself obeyed from one end of the world to the other? his name, his signature, has no necessity, like the army of a Sovereign, for the value of metal to come to the assistance of the impression: himself does all; he has signed, and that is enough.'

Lord Munster replied, 'that there were two ranks in life he should prefer as more suitable to the title he bore, though unaccompanied by fortune, the magistrate who supports the laws, or that of the soldier who defends his country!' Highly charmed with his sentiments, it required no small resolution for his aunt, who fondly loved him, to support the character she had assumed;

* See Duhalde's description of China.

† In opposition to this, noblemen and men of fortune bred at the Dublin University, are excused from learning morality, as they can graduate without any skill in that science; the professor making no doubt, but that honesty necessarily springs up with nobility. The same University refused Swift his degree of *Batchelor of Arts for dulness and insufficiency*, but he at last obtained it *Speciali gratia*.

‡ This Lady Frances entertained no fears about: A French author justly observes, *Jamais on ne prend les vices d'une condition au dessous de la sienne: L'enfant du riche, par un sentiment d'orgueil, bauffe les épaules sur les defauts du pauvre.*

but recollecting herself, observed, that it was not unusual for men of high birth to enrich their family *by trade*.

When the Earl of Oxford was at the head of affairs in England, his brother was a factor at Aleppo; and if Lord Townshend was respected in parliament as a secretary of state, his brother was no less regarded in the city as a merchant. Without giving way, added she, to ideas of birth, you may be happy, and by your temper, application, and personal accomplishments, make a figure in life without the aid of such an accidental *appendage*; and by your attainments and engaging qualities obtain a general esteem, the surest step to advancement and honor.

Lord Munster seemed *convinced*, though not allured by her arguments, yielding himself to her guidance, with that sweetness of disposition, which though so amiable in itself is so much to be apprehended. For those dispositions of the mind, which are generally termed virtuous, are frequently the occasion of our falling into vices, from which opposite ones, though generally condemned, would have secured us.

In pursuance of Lady Frances's plan, Lord Munster was sent to Holland, where he was boarded for two years in a creditable family in Amsterdam, as the best school for learning, temperance, economy, and every domestic virtue.

Men of all climates and religions being also natives of Holland, gave him liberal notions and enlarged ideas; their earth is as free as their air. Their toleration of religion, indeed, is so extreme, it amounts to a total unconcern about them. At the same communion, in the same church, some receive sitting, others standing, or kneeling; and this freedom appeared to that crafty people, such unquestionable policy, that it came in from common sense alone, and passed without a law.* To this cause is assigned the number of inhabitants; as the land fit for tillage in Holland does not exceed four hundred thousand acres‡. This country in

* The Empress Catharine II, whose name will be immortal, gave a code of laws to her empire, which contains a fifth part of the globe; and the first of her laws was to establish universal toleration. In France foreign protestants are admitted to all the rights of natives after working for a certain time in the manufactory of the Gobelines. The same policy has been adopted by the Spaniards.

‡ Ruben's pictures are *a toleration of all religions*. In one of the compartments of the Luxemburgh gallery, a cardinal introduces Mercury to Mary de Medicis, and Hymen supports her train at the sacrament of marriage, before an altar, on which are the images of God the Father, and Christ.

itself furnishes an illustration of the plan Lady Frances was following with her nephew. Industry, honesty, and concern for the public welfare, made the inhabitants considerable. If they depart from these, and if the sea returns upon them, their having existed will be known only from tradition and books. The preservation of both Egypt and Holland depends upon the care they take of their dykes, and canals; but there is no work in the former so great as the building such a city as Amsterdam upon piles in the sea*. Venice also furnishes a striking instance of what wonders may be effected by industry: that out of a morass, a city of such splendor could be raised, and become the emporium of Europe, as it was before the discovery of the East and West Indies, is extraordinary. But this trade decayed, as that of Holland increased: almost all merchandizes which came from the Mediterranean were formerly landed at Venice, and from thence brought to Augsburg; from which place, they were dispersed through all Germany. But Holland has taken away all, and distributes all; and Augsburg suffers, as well as Venice, Milan, Antwerp, and an infinite number of other cities, which are at *present* as *poor* as *formerly* they *were rich*. This furnishes an excellent example of the benefits arising from industry, and the necessity of exertion. Lord Munster rendered himself entirely master of the knowledge of our English trade and privileges. He also attained a competent skill in the history of jurisprudence†. As it is requisite for every man who has leisure and capacity for such researches to be acquainted with the nature and extent of that judicial authority which is to decide upon his person and property, and to which as a citizen he is bound to submit, he studied the English constitution and government in the ancient books of common law, and more modern writers, who out

---

* As both are against nature, she in the end will get the better of them. The modern philosophers of Sweden seem agreed that the waters of the Baltic gradually sink in a regular proportion, which they have ventured to estimate at half an inch every year. – Twenty centuries ago, the flat country of Scandinavia must have been covered by the sea; such is the notion given us by Mela, Pliny, and Tacitus, of the vast countries round the Baltic. Adria, that ancient and famous city, which gave its name to the Gulph is now but a pitiful half drowned village.

† See Gilbert's treatise on the Court of Exchequer, chap. 2. well worthy the perusal of those who would be acqainted with the foundation of our constitution: also Mr de Lolme's book on the English Constitution, which has been mentioned in both houses of parliament, and has been commented on, and quoted by, the most celebrated writers of every party.

of them have given an account of this government. He next proceeded to the history of England, and with it joined in every king's reign the laws then made —— This gave him insight into the reason of our statutes, and shewed him the true ground upon which they came to be made, and what weight they ought to have. By this means he read the history of his own country with intelligence, and was able to examine into the *excellence* or *defects* of its *government*, and to judge of the *fitness* or *unfitness* of its *orders* and *laws*: and by this method he knows enough of the English law for a gentleman, though quite ignorant of the *chicane* or wrangling, and captious part of it, or the arts how to *avoid* doing *right*, and to *secure himself* in *doing wrong*. As Lord Munster was now eighteen years of age, Lady Frances wrote and acquainted him, that as he had rather testified a dislike to the mercantile scheme, she desired he would relinquish it; and as nothing contributes more to enlighten and improve the understanding, than a pesonal acquaintance with foreign climates, she desired he would travel. – The man who by his birth-right is a free member of society, not a slave to despotic power, and who, in matters of religion, enjoys the invaluable blessing of private judgment, should not fail to visit other nations; for this will not only rub off all the selfish asperities he may have contracted from a narrow survey of things, but will also accompany him home with a more rational attachment to that constitution under which he had the happiness to be born. Heaven has placed us in a most advantageous situation; unless we are divided at home, attacks from abroad may molest but cannot ruin us. Our laws are the laws of freedom; our merchandise the traffic of opulence —— Our constitution is framed and joined together by the choicest parts, picked and extracted from aristocracies, democracies, and sovereignties. We have a natural force to *defend* and *maintain* the empire of the seas. We enjoy wealth and possessions in both the Indies, if we do not lose them by our own misconduct —— We boast at regular choice, and singular system of parliamentary government, so nicely calculated, as to be at once the defence and the support of the kingdom and the people. Our Sovereign has the power – but the parliament has still the law of that power*. – What people on earth can say the same? The studies Lord Munster made of our

---

* See Bacon on government.

constitution, when contrasted with his observations of other countries, made him return after three years, not a *nominal*, but a *real* patriot. This is not always the case. Too many of our young gentlemen bring home only a miserable reverse of every good purpose for which they were sent out:– as none travel more than the English, they ought, therefore, to let none surpass them in manly or generous perceptions. But we have reason to fear that what Mr Pope observes of *one* of them may be applicable to *most*.

'Europe he saw, and Europe saw him too.'

Is not this owing to their early visiting France, where slavery is so artfully gilded over as to hide its natural deformity? If our countrymen were first to make the tour of Denmark, where the people are more apparently slaves, it would remedy this evil. On the contrary, when the subject of an arbitrary government has travelled into countries which enjoy the inestimable advantages of civil and religious liberty, he returns with a diminished affection for his own, and learns to despise and dislike that constitution which denies him the enjoyment of those natural rights, the knowledge and the value of which he has learnt from his happier neighbours.

Hence it is that despotic princes are cautious how they permit their subjects to *range abroad*; and for the reasons above intimated, travelling has ever been encouraged in free states.

With the finest person, Lord Munster possessed all the virtues and the graces —— was all complacency in his manners, all sweetness in his disposition; humane, susceptible, and compassionate.

While Lady Frances had taken so much care of his education, it may be readily supposed she was not forgetful of Lady Eliza's, his sister – whose person is faultless, and of the middle size – her face is a sweet oval, and her complexion the *brunette* of the bright kind. The finest passions are always passing in her face; and in her lovely eyes there is a fluid fire sufficient to animate a score of inanimate beauties. She has a clear understanding, and a sound judgment; has read a great deal, and has a most happy elocution: possesses a great share of wit, and with equal strength and propriety can express the whole series of the passions in comic characters. The pliableness of her dispositions can raise and keep up agreeable sensations, and amuse her company.

Lord L——— declares he never saw anything equal to her,

even on the French stage, in the article of transition from passion to passion in comic life. She is perfect mistress of music, and plays admirably well on the harpsicord; having great neatness, and more expression and meaning in her playing, than is often found among lady-players. – In this, as in every other branch of her education, she has had every advantage – Lady Frances herself being highly accomplished – and her long residence in Italy and France having perfected and improved her taste, in every accomplishment that can embellish or add graces to the youth and beauty of her niece – All her musical band have been the pupils of the first masters, and recommended to her by Santirelli, Jomelli, Galuppi, Piccini, and Sacchini. It is not then surprising that the works of these different masters are performed admirably well at Munster-house; and as there is great variety in their manner, there is that in every one of them to charm and please the most insensible. Lady Frances is highly charmed with Jomelli; while the fancy, fire, and feeling of Galuppi, and Piccini's comic stile, are infinitely more attracting to Lady Eliza, than the taste, learning, great and noble ideas of Jomelli, or the serious stile of Sacchini. – One of the Bezzodzi's, from Turin who excells on the hautboy, is also at Munster-house.

There is also a set of very excellent actors, who perform at the Tribuna, judging the representation of dramatic works of genius contribute as much to soften manners, as the exhibition of the Gladiators formerly did to harden them. When we complain of the *licentiousness* of the stage, I fear we have more reason to complain of *bad measures* in our policy, and a general decay of *virtue* and *good morals* among us.

Moliere's comedies are said to have done more service to the courtiers, than the sermons of Bourdalone and Massillon. The great Saint Chrysostom, a name consecrated to immortality by his virtue, is thought to owe a great part of his eloquence and vehemence in correcting vice, to his constantly reading Aristophanes; nor was he even censured on that account, in those times of pure zeal, and primitive religion.

Lord Shaftesbury says, 'Bigotry hurries us away into the most furious excesses, upon trifles of no manner of consequence.' What is more useful to a nation than the picture of strong passions, and their fatal effects; of great crimes, and their chastisement; of great virtues, and their reward? Scarce had Peter the Great polished

Russia, before theatres were established there. The more
Germany has improved, the more of our dramatic representations
has it adopted. Those few places, where they were not received in
the last age, are never ranked among civilized countries: and
theatrical entertainments have their use everywhere, and often
keep the common people from a worse employment of their
time – and so far were the institution of theatres from being the
fore-runners of slavery, or the badges of despotism, that they were
most encouraged, and flourished best in free states.

It is easy to conceive that the acquaintance of Lady Frances was
much courted, as no private person had it so much in their power
to entertain their company so well; there being every requisite at
Munster-house to delight the heart, please the eyes, and satisfy
the understanding. – No person of any taste but would blush to
acknowledge they have not been in Shropshire to admire her
buildings, manufactures, schools etc. – And it fares with her merit
like the pictures of Raphael, which are seen with admiration by all,
or at least no one dare own that he has no taste for a composition
which has received so universal an applause.

Upon Lord Munster's being of age, she was thirty-seven; yet
the regularity of her life contributed to make her lose no more in
her person than what might be considered as the slight touches in
a picture, which when faded diminish nothing of the master-
strokes of the piece. Lord Darnley, since the time he had expected
to become Lady Frances's husband, still continued to attach
himself to her. 'Whatever her determinations may be,' said he, 'I
am sensible of the value of her soul; her friendship is more tender
than the endearment of love in other women.' Such forbearances
were not uncommon in ages of chivalry; and however justly
ridiculed by the inimitable *Cervantes*, when carried to extremes,
and terminating in Quixotism, yet it appears to constitute a capital
part of the character of *a true* knight. Lord Darnley's attachment
to Lady Frances was not founded on the weakness of his intellects;
it never made him forgetful of his duties to society. He is at the
same time a philosopher and a politician; and adds practice to
speculation, experience to knowledge, in both these departments.
Though the brilliant actions of some heroes are only handed down
to us, and we view their characters through the magnifying end of
the tube, yet Hercules himself could lay aside his club, and amuse
himself with the distaff, to enjoy the company of the woman he

loved. All great souls have descended occasionally, and divesting themselves of their heroism, have become susceptible of the *tender passion*.

Lady Frances respected Lord Darnley's character, as much as she loved his person; and the time was now arrived when she proposed ingenuously to confess to him the reasons of her past conduct, and to offer to dedicate the remainder of her life in rewarding his tender, fond, faithful attentions. But she suspected that – years had made such an alteration in her person, that she ceased to be an object *of love*, (to his lordship) although perfectly convinced she possessed *his esteem* – Under this apprehension it became impossible for her to act the part she intended – She became disquieted, and was determined, had that really been the case, never to have allied herself to any other. After revolving a thousand things, she at last determined to confirm or confute her hopes, by employing a particular friend, and a relation of Lord Darnley's, to discover his sentiments. Lady Frances's intimacy with this lady had commenced at Paris, when they were in the convent of the ———— . As her character is peculiar, the indulgent reader will perhaps pardon the introduction of her story in this place.

At the time Lady Frances returned to England, Mrs Lee was taken out of the convent to be married. Her parents, dazzled with Mr Lee's wealth, forgot to attend to other requisites to render that state happy. Without his being a man of very shining parts, he had such talents as made him acceptable to women, in particular to a girl so young as she was when this alliance took place. He sung and danced well, was lively to extravagance, full of agreeable trifling, and always in good humour: add to this, he was handsome in his person, liberal to excess, and calculated for the seduction of the fair. Mrs Lee's great beauty, her parents partially flattered themselves would fix his affections. – All the graces of which the figure and emotions of a female were capable, were united in her; but his love for her was nothing but an impulse of passion which soon subsided. Addicted by his natural disposition to pleasure, he despised those which a tender sensibility renders so exquisitely delightful; such would have trespassed too much on his vanity. Unexperienced and artless, his innocent wife could not long retain his affections, and in the few years she lived with him, encountered many mortifications; first from the alienation of his affections, afterwards from the distressed situation of his affairs, which entirely changed his temper, rendering him impatient and passionate. His very footmen were taught to insult her, and every one in the family knew the most effectual way to ingratiate themselves with him, was to disregard his wife. Yet she bore it all with patience, and acted her part with prudence, endeavouring to disarm his anger with gentleness. She sometimes, indeed, lamented and complained, but the dove and the lamb do so too – 'The poison of grief exhales only in complaints.' – She was neither sullen nor gay when he was out of humour; nor impertinent or melancholy when he was pleased – She obliged her affections to wait and submit to the various turns of his temper – trying to bribe his passions to her interest. She endeavoured also, by economy and proper attention, to retard as long as possible, the ruin that threatened him; and considerably diminished the household expenses.

This pleased her husband; he wanted to retrench, without appearing less magnificent; for his prudence (or rather his desire of saving at home to squander abroad) was still subordinate to his ostentation. But all these innocent stratagems were ineffectual; spending his whole time between women, racing, and gaming, one excess succeeded another, until his affairs were intirely involved. Previous to this, Mrs Lee had resigned her jewels to pay one of his game debts, which she afterwards saw adorning a girl he kept. The world saw he devoted himself only to objects of contempt, and pitied his neglect of a woman of her merit, and who was still handsome, having that style of beauty which is the image of a sensible heart, though sorrow and tears had deprived it of its freshness. This laid her open to the assiduity of men of gallantry, who are generally obliging enough, upon such occasions, to offer their assistance to dry up a *pretty woman's tears*. It is to be confessed a woman under these circumstances is in a very *dangerous situation*.

None of Mr Lee's conduct was founded on propriety — he was witty, kind, cold, angry, easy, stiff, jealous, careless, cautious, confident, close, open, but all *in the wrong place*. She often retired into her closet, and wept the silent hours away for his hard-heartedness – yet without one unkind word or reproach. Her parents were dead, Lady Frances at a distance, her sorrows of a complicated kind, which required great delicacy to discover; she had no person to open her heart to, none to whom she could pour forth the sorrows of the soul! she had a susceptible heart, and no object she took any interest in, or who participated in her trials. – This situated, (the candid must acknowledge) she was perhaps more to be *pitied* than *blamed*, in permitting another object to glide insensibly into her affections — more especially as he was introduced by Mr Lee, as one to whom she was indebted for his life and fortune.

The first he had defended, when two gamblers, his adversaries, were on the point of killing him; *the last* he had preserved by discovering a scheme that had been practised on him by them when inebriated by liquor, to which he was much addicted. Her husband left her young and unexperienced heart to all the tortures and pangs of jealousy, and that *ennui* attending an unoccupied heart; after flattering herself, as she had done nothing to deserve the estrangement of his affections, that they would be as permanent as her own. Why did he forsake her; why did he lay her open to temptations? her heart might have been his own, had he not cruelly abandoned her — at any rate it was too good to form another tye, had he not at last added *contempt* to *neglect* and his cruel usage at last would have animated a statue, at least I may safely declare nothing warmed with flesh and blood could bear it. A man of this humour is to be beloved only in the way of christianity — that is the utmost obedience which can be allowed to the commandments of God, and the authority of religion.

Were I obliged to draw a picture that should represent the happy union between an elevated soul, a penetrating mind, and a heart in which sweet humanity resides, I would form it entirely of the person and features of Mr Villars; and I fancy that all who had any just idea of those three qualities might perceive them plainly expressed in his form, look, and demeanor. Mr Lee pressed him to be much at his house; and as his *innocent*, though *oppressed*, wife had been kept in constant alarms concerning the consequences of his gaming —— she could not but look on Mr Villars as the favour of her fortune, and on one to whom she might be indebted for her husband's reformation. I shall not expatiate on the sweetness and charms of his voice, of his noble appearance, and of the tincture of melancholy which softens the vivacity of his fine eyes; but what distinguishes him from most other men is the sentimental look of modest virtue, which never gives offence. He is not in the least a slave to interest; but as he is no stranger to the necessities of life, his conduct is always regular, and he never abandons himself to any excess. Such is and was Mr Villars. Mrs Lee very soon perceived his partiality for her – circumstanced as she was, his attentions were dangerous – but she could not with any propriety forbid him *a house* to which her husband so constantly *invited him*, without letting him see she mistrusted herself – more especially as he never failed in his respect for her.

He became her only comforter and friend; and if from her youth and inexperience she was likely to fall into even the appearance of any error, it was this kind, this friendly monitor that guarded her from it.

His attentions became as necessary to her soul, as aliments of food are to the support of the body, while the respectful distance of his behaviour proved to her his passion was controlled by his respect.

Some surmises were at length insinuated to Mr Lee, to his wife's dishonour. He paid little attention to them – but coming home one night flushed with wine, and finding Mr Villars alone at supper with her, (no unusual matter, and by his own request) he drew his sword, and wounded him before he had time to defend himself! Mrs Lee fainted away —— on her recovery she removed herself from a house to which no entreaties on his part could prevail on her to return – declaring she would live no longer with a man who could at once suspect her virtue, endanger his friend's life, and ruin her reputation.

The world talked differently about this affair. Should not the example of the law be followed, which is so tender in criminal cases, that delinquents are often found *not guilty*, for want of legal evidence, at the same time that the court, the jury, and every one present at the trial feel the strongest *moral* conviction of their *guilt?* Scandal on the contrary always gives its most important and fatal decisions from *appearances* and *suppositions*, though reputation is dearer to a woman of honor than life itself. Mrs Lee experienced the malevolence of her own sex particularly. What, said they, could engage Mr Villars to devote all his time to her? is not friendship between a man and a woman a chimera, the mark of a passion which honor or self-interest bids them conceal? But whilst the world represented this affair in the worst colours, Lady Frances wrote her an affectionate letter, offering her assistance, and begging she would communicate her real situation, that she might the more effectually be enabled to serve her; to which Mrs Lee returned the following answer.

    'Dear Madam.

I received the honor of your letter, and find myself elevated by your notice – if there can be pride that ranks with virtues, it is that we feel from friendships with the worthy. The liberal senitments you express, are a proof of the goodness of your heart —— I have ever thought that to believe the worst is a mark of a mean spirit, and a wicked soul; at least I am sure, that the contrary quality, when it is not due to weakness of understanding, is the fruit of a generous temper. In return for your generosity, I will lay open my whole heart to you; and if in consequence I lose your esteem, I shall at least have the satisfaction resulting from a consciousness of my candour. This is a liberty I should have taken before, had it not proceeded from the timidity I felt in unbosoming myself to one whose virtues I dreaded, and in discovering *my weakness* to one who I think has *none of her own*. Your ladyship knows the trials I suffered for many years; my conduct under the severest mortifications human nature could sustain. I was wounded in my affections, condemned and insulted in my person, impoverished in my circumstances: I still had strength of mind to regulate myself so as to meet your approbation: no species of calamity was unknown to me, nor were there wanting those of the other sex, who judged from my situation they might have a chance of succeeding with me, if I was weak enough to listen to them – but they soon gave up the pursuit, judging the excess of my misfortunes had hardened my heart entirely against certain impressions. But this was so far from being the case, that my sorrows, my sufferings, rendered my heart (naturally tender) more susceptible of that refined passion, which, when dignified by respect, and softened by tenderness, found so ready access to it*.

---

* I lately met with the following story, which affected me very much, and which I give in the original; it elucidates, that a return of affection seems absolutely necessary to the existence of the human heart. 'Un homme respectable, après avoir joué un grand rôle à Paris, y vivoit dans un reduit obscur, victime de l'infortune, et si indigent qu'il ne subsistoit que des aumônes de la paroisse; on lui remettoit par

cont'd over

In short, circumstanced as I was, if it is a crime to love, I am very culpable! but had I unfortunately proceeded to any act contrary to my engagements with Mr Lee, I myself would have acquainted him with it, though, in the opinion of many, he would not have deserved so much candour from me.

This being the real state of the case, I flatter myself your ladyship will think me more *weak* than *wicked*, more *frail* than *culpable*, more *unfortunate* than *indiscreet*. And I must now acquaint you, that I am determined never to return to my husband – I have consulted my reason on this subject, and when we have done so, whatever the decision be, whether in favour of our prejudices, or against them, we must rest satisfied, since nothing can be more certain than this, that he who follows that guide in the search of truth, as that was given to direct him, will have a much better plea to make for his conduct, than he who has resigned himself implicitly to the guidance of others. My maxim is, our understanding, *properly* exercised, is the *medium* by which God makes known his *will* to us; and that in all *cases*, the voice of impartial reason is the *voice of* God. Were my marriage even to be annulled, all the theologians in the world could not prove the least impiety in it. – Milton wrote *the doctrine and discipline of divorce*; wherein he proves, that a contrariety of mind, destructive of felicity, peace, and happiness, are greater reasons of divorce than adultery, especially if there be no children, and there be a mutual consent for separation

He dedicated the second edition to the parliament of England, with the assembly of divines —— The latter summoned him before the house of Lords, who, whether

---

semaine la quantité du pain suffisante pour sa nourriture; il en fit demander davantage; le curé lui écrit pour l'engager à passer chez lui; il vient. Le curè s'informe s'il vit seul; et avec qui, Monsieur, repond-il, voudriez-vous que je vécasse? je suis malheureux, vous le voyez, puis que j'ai recours à charitè, et tout le monde m'a abandonné, tout le monde! Mais, Monsieur, continue le curé, si vous êtes seul, pourquoi demandez vous plus de pain que ce qui vous est necessaire? L'autre paroit déconcerté; il avoue avec peine qu'il a un chien: le curé ne le laisse pas poursuivre; il lui fait observer qu'il n'est que le distributeur du pain des pauvres, et que l'honneteté exige absolument qu'il se defasse de son chien. Eh! Monsieur, s'ecrie en pleurant l'infortune, si je m'en défais, qui est ce qui m'aimera? Le pasteur attendri jusqu'aux larmes, tire sa bourse, et la lui donne, en disant, Prenez, Monsieur ceci m'appartient.'

approving his doctrine, or not favouring his accusers, dismissed him. Necessary and just causes have necessary and just consequences: what error and disaster joined, reason and equity should disjoin.

I see no reason why those who upon the evidence of more than fourteen years experience are unsuited to each other, *joined* not *matched*, should live disagreeably together, and exist miserably – merely for the inadequate satisfaction of exulting upon the degree of their patience in having to say they did *not part*. A person may mistake in fixing love without knowledge of the party, but he cannot err that finds cause to dislike from woeful experience. It is, indeed, convenient for the lords of the creation to inculcate another doctrine, upon the same principles that the extreme and timorous attention to his own security made James I. very anxious to infuse into his subjects the belief of divine hereditary right, and a scrupulous unreserved obedience *to the power which God had set over them*. Mr Villars, who is now reconciled with my husband, has written to intercede in his behalf, assuring me of his penitence and affection. Boileau has observed, that it is an easy matter in a *Christian poem* for *God* to bring the *devil to reason*. Could I believe that all my husband did, were the effects of love, it would not in the least alter my resolution, since I should consider a person whose affection had such dreadful effects, as dangerous to my repose, as one whose anger was implacable. —— What signifies it to me whether it be love or hatred by which I suffer, if the danger and inconvenience be the same? I am certain were we to live together again, whenever we met we should as naturally quarrel as the elephant and the rhinoceros. Reconciliations in the marriage state, after violent breaches, are seldom lasting, and after what has passed between us, like the father of the gods and the queen of heaven, we shall be the best company when *asunder*.

He says his conduct proceeded from an excess of love! I desire to be subject no more to such excesses! I am content to be moderately beloved; nor shall I ever again give occasion for such extraordinary proofs of affection. Were I to act otherwise, it would afford too much encouragement for the men to use their wives ill. *Too good subjects are apt to make bad kings*. He has my consent to live with any woman who can delight in such a *loving husband*, while I will force him to esteem my conduct, and irritate his animosity by declining a reconciliation. We are tired with perpetual gratitude, and perpetual hatred. —— He wishes to be reconciled to me, not from any religious motive, or return of affection, his animosity being still the same – but because he is tired of acting the part of a provoked husband.

I am piqued at Mr Villars's interesting himself in this matter. I shall not answer his letter for a week; I mistrust my own vivacity.

Our imagination is often our greatest enemy: I am striving to weary mine before I act. Business like fruit hath its time of maturity, and we should not think of dispatching it while it is half ripe. The Cardinal de Retz said, 'I have all my life-time held men in greater esteem for what they forbore to do on some occasions than for what they did.'

I have here a most delightful dwelling —— It is thatched, and covered on every side with roses, wood-bines, and honey-suckles, surrounded with a garden of the most artful confusion. The streams all around murmur, and fall a thousand ways. A great variety of birds are here collected, and are in high harmony on the sprays. The ruins of an abbey enhance the beauties of this place: they appear at the distance of four hundred yards from the house; and as some great trees are now grown up among the remains, and a river winds among the broken walls, the view is solemn, the picture fine. Here I often meditate on my misfortunes.

> 'There is a joy in grief when peace dwells
> in the breast of the sad.'
>
> OSSIAN'S Poems.

Sadness receives so many eulogiums in the scripture, that it is easy to judge, that if it be not of the number of the, virtues it may be usefully employed in their service —— and it may be truly observed, that without experiencing sorrow, we should never know life's true value.

About a mile above the house is a range of very high hills, the sight of which renders me less incredulous of the accounts of Olympus, and mount Athos. Hygeia resides here, and dispenses the chief blessings of life, ease and health. I will pass my days in sweet tranquillity and study.

'In either place 'tis folly to complain,
The mind, and not the place, creates the pain.'
HORACE, lib. I. epist. 14.

Could I flatter myself I should ever be honored by your presence, how happy I should be! —— Your eye, I am sure, would catch pleasure while it measures the surrounding landscape (even at this season of the year) of russet lawns and grey fallows, on which stray the nibbling flocks: the mountains too, which seem to support the labouring clouds, add sublimity to the charming scene. When I take a walk after a sedentary occupation, I feel a sensible pleasure; rest in its turn becomes agreeable, if it has been preceded by a moderate fatigue. Every action of our lives may be converted into a kind of pleasure, if it is but well timed: Life owes all its joys to this well-adapted succession; and he will never enjoy its true relish, who does not know to blend pleasure with dissipation. I ask pardon for detaining your ladyship so long – My cousin Lord Darnley has been to see, and admires my cottage. – I perceive plainly he flatters himself that you will one day make him happy. I do not presume to offer my advice; it would be imitating the savage chief, who marks out to the sun the course it is to take —— but surely his respectful, uninterrupted attachment deserves your consideration. Were I not perfectly convinced of his worth and sincerity, I should be *the last* person to speak in his behalf. The bitterness of conjugal repentance, which I have experienced, is beyond all others poignant; and happy it is if *disunion*, rather than perpetual *disagreement*, results from it.

I ever am your ladyship's
Obliged and affectionate friend,

LUCY LEE.'

Lady Frances returned Mrs Lee immediately the following answer.

'Dear Madam,   Munster-house.

I return you many thanks for the confidence you honored
me with; and I sincerely sympathize with you on the many
disagreeable events that have occurred to you. If my
approbation can confer on you any satisfaction, you possess it
in a very eminent degree: for though I cannot approve of your
sentiments concerning divorce, etc. yet your conduct in your
family was exemplary.

There is no reasoning about the motions of the heart.
Reflection and sensation are extremely different – our affections are not in our own power, though yours seem to have
been under proper regulations.

I am not surprised at the calumny you met with. Many
people stoop to the baseness of discovering in a person
distinguished by eminent qualities, the weaknesses of humanity, while there is scarcely to be found an honest heart, who
knows how to render a noble and sincere homage to another's
superiority. I acknowledge myself guilty with respect to you,
of a too common instance of injustice, that of desiring that
others would always *conduct themselves* by our maxims! I am
the more culpable, as I entirely agree with you in thinking
that all our actions should proceed from the fixed principles
we have adopted. I never pay a blind deference to the
judgment of any man, or any body of men whatever. I cannot
acquiesce in a decision, however formidable made by
numbers, where my own reason is not satisfied. When the
mind has no *data*, no settled principles to which it may recur
as the rule of action, the agent can feel little or no satisfaction
within himself, and society can have no moral security
whatever against him.

The most permanent, the most pleasing enjoyment the
human soul is capable of entertaining, is that which arises
from a consciousness of having acted up to that standard of
rectitude which we conceive to be the proper measure of our
duty: and the best grounds on which we can expect others to
place confidence in us, is the assurance we give them that we
act under the influence of such moral obligations. This
principle has influenced my conduct: and as you say you are
absolutely determined never to live with your husband again;

although my sentiments do not correspond with yours on that head, I will add nothing further on that subject, but refer you to certain passages in scripture, which I think on sober reflection must invalidate your present opinion*.

The caprice you have often tacitly blamed me for respecting Lord Darnley, had you known the motives for, you would have approved – I will now in reward for your candour *to me* be equally sincere *with you* – trusting to your honor, that you will not *divulge* what is it so material to me to *conceal*.

At the time I agreed to give Lord Darnley my hand, I was at liberty to indulge my inclinations, and to devote myself entirely to him: But on my father's death, when I found the estate in my possession, I considered myself as mother to my brother's children. This was my motive for rejecting the man I (*did*, and do *now*) fondly love: who by his generous and friendly, his respectful and tender behaviour, deserves every thing from me. Whoever pretends to be without passions, censures the wisdom of that Power which made him; and if men of sense (for they alone are capable of refined pleasure) would so far admit love, as not to exclude their necessary and more important duties, they need not be ashamed to indulge one of the most valuable blessings of an innocent life. I honor the married state: and have high ideas of the happiness resulting from an union of hearts. Domestic society is founded on the union betwixt husband and wife. Among all the civilized nations, this union hath been esteemed sacred and honorable; and from it are derived those exquisite joys, or sorrows, which can embitter all the pleasures, or alleviate all the pains in human life. The heart has but a certain degree of sensibility, which we ought to be economists of. Lord Darnley engrossed my whole soul; nothing could afford me any pleasure which had no reference to him. – He was ever uppermost in my thoughts, and I bestowed only a secondary reflection on all other subjects.

I could have cheerfully, for his *conversation*, abandoned all society on earth beside, and have been more blessed, than if, for them, I had been deprived of *his*. But if we suffer one particular duty (even the worship of the Deity) to engross us

* Chap. of St. Mark. XVI Chap. of St. Luke. VII Chap. of the Romans.

entirely, or even to encroach upon the rest, we make but a very imperfect essay towards religion, or virtue; and are still at a considerable distance from the business of a moral agent. "The dial that mistells one hour, of consequence is false through the whole round of day."

Virtue, in my acceptation, is nothing else than that principle by which our actions are *intentionally directed*, to produce good, to the several objects of our free agency. I was aware, that it was not only necessary that I should mean to act a right part, and take the best way which could direct me to effect it, but that I should previously take those measures which were in my power to acquire the knowledge of my duty, and of the weaknesses I had to guard against. I was sensible, that, had I given my hand to Lord Darnley, I would have been defective in the duties incumbent on me to my own family:– Love would have taken entire possession of my soul, and shut up the avenues of my heart against every other sentiment. Upon this occasion I felt how justly the sacrifice of our own happiness is placed among the highest virtues. How painful must it be to the most generous heart! Men lose their lives to honor – I relinquished my love – the life of life. I am sensible I have been condemned for permitting him to be so much with me: but what recompence can the world bestow on me, for relinquishing the society of a real and tender friend? Common attachments, the shadows of friendship, the issue of chance, or fantastic likings, *rashly cemented*, may as hastily be *dissolved*: but mine has had the purest virtue for its basis, and will subsist whilst vital breath in me remains. My affections are founded on those amiable qualities, which are seldom united, and therefore but little liable to be displaced. My partiality is founded on esteem: take away the cause, the effect will cease. The dread of the world has never yet withheld me from following the bent of my own inclinations, and the dictates of my own heart, not the dread of censure ever influenced my conduct.

Your mention of his continued attachment is highly flattering, and very pleasing – There you touched the tenderest springs of my heart, bring me down to all the softness of my sex, and press upon me a crowd of tender, lovely, ideas –

If the consciousness of good-will to others, though inactive, be highly delightful, what a superior joy have I not experienced, my dear friend, in exerting this disposition, in acts of beneficence! Is not this the supereme enjoyment in nature? It is true, the great works I have carried on, the encouragement I have given to learning, the manufactories I have introduced into this kingdom, etc. etc. have procured me the suffrage of the world, and may transmit my name down to posterity. But what flatters me most is, that if I have acquired any fame, it is derived from the man I love. My acquaintance with him, has been a happiness to my mind, because it has improved and exalted its powers. The epithet of *great*, so liberally bestowed on princes, would, in most cases, if narrowly scanned, belong rather to their ministers. Unassisted by Agrippa and Mecænas, where should we have placed Augustus? What is the history of Lewis XIII. but the shining acts of Richelieu? Lewis XIV. was indeed a great king; but the Condés, the Turennes, as well as the Luvois, and Colberts, had no small share in acquiring the glories of his reign. In all situations of life, it is of great consequence to make a right choice of those we confide in – It is on that choice our own glory and peace depend. – But it is still more so to princes, or persons of large property. A private man will find a thousand persons ready to open his eyes, by reproaching him with the wrong steps into which bad advice drew him; whereas courtiers, or those who are interested, approve and applaud whatever the prince or the great person does. An ingenious courtier replied to his friend, who upbraided him with his too great complaisance for the emperor who had made bad verses, which he commended; "Would you have me have more sense than a man who commands twelve legions, and can banish me?"

That day my nephew is of age, I shall assign over his estate, and acquaint him of his obligations to Lord Darnley, to whom, at the same time, I shall offer my hand, if I have reason then to think it shall be agreeable to him. If it should not, I shall be mortified, though I shall not deck my brow with the plaintive willow. I need not tell you how agreeable it will be for me to see you at this place, which is considerably improved since you were here last. This day month I give a feast, in imitation of the Saturnalia*; make me happy by your presence on that occasion.

    I remain, with great esteem,
      Your affectionate friend,

                          FRANCES FINLAY.

Mrs Lee, soon after the receipt of the above letter, came to Munster-house, where she generally resided during the winter months, (after her separation from her husband) retiring to her cottage in Wales, in the summer.

Lady Frances had always a select number of friends with her. Notwithstanding her passion for music, she kept the performers in their own line; and though she venerated the liberal sciences, and contributed so largely to their cultivation, their several professors only waited on her by invitation: by this means she had it always in her power to suit her company, and never to be intruded on; as the best things are irksome to those whose inclinations, tastes, and humours, they do not suit.

I have already mentioned Mrs Norden, who had the care of Lady Frances's education, and who now continued ro reside with her: this Lady's seriousness was happily contrasted with Lady Eliza's sprightliness, while Lady Frances's scientifical knowledge was agreeably relieved by the strokes of nature observable in Mrs Lee – who declared she had never read, or studied, any more than to assist her decyphering what was incumbent her *to understand*. 'I hate your wise ones,' said she, 'there is no opinion so absurd but it has been mentioned by some philosopher.' She is nature itself, without disguise, quite original disdaining all imitation, even in her dress, which is simple but unaffected. She plays most divinely on the fiddle. Her genius for music is sublime and universal. She holds the fiddle like a man, and produces music in all its genuine charms, raising the soul into the finest affections.

An aunt and sister of Sir Harry Bingley's were also much at Munster-house. Miss Bingley was of the same age with Lady Eliza: to the charms of a regular beauty she joins all those of a cultivated mind, together with a disposition replete with candor, and a turn for ridicule; two things rarely joined together – as a calm dispassionate love of truth, with a disposition to examine

* Which was upheld in Heathen Rome, about the time we keep our Christmas.

carefully, and judge impartially, with a love of diverting one's self at other people's expense, seldom meet together in the same mind. Mrs Dorothea Bingley is a maiden lady of fifty, possessed of a large independent fortune, which she proposes to bestow on her niece. She was in her youth very handsome: but having lived all her life in the country, she derived all her ideas of love from the heroic romance. To talk to her of love was a capital offence. Her rigour must be melted by the blood of giants, necromancers, and paynim knights. She expected, that, for her sake, they would retire to desarts, mourn her cruelty, *subsist* on *nothing*; and make light of scampering over impassable mountains, and riding through unfordable rivers, without recollecting, that, while the imagination of the lover is linked to this *muddy vesture of decay*, she must now and then condescend to partake of the carnality of the vivres of the shambles.

Those of the other sex who were mostly at Munster-house, were, Lord Darnley, Sir Harry Bingley, Sir James Mordaunt, etc. etc. etc. Great marriages had been proposed to Lady Frances; but she had ceased long to be importuned on that head. When Lord Munster was of age she gave a splendid entertainment to the neighbourhood, which finished with a ball. The day after she shewed her nephew the state of her affairs, when she succeeded to the estate: and that, exclusive of the buildings, etc. etc. she had already doubled it: that the perpetual burdens she had entailed on it, did not amount to one quarter of the advanced rents, which would continue to encrease: that she had put aside for Lady Eliza's fortune fifty thousand pounds, and an equivalent sum for herself, and then with great pleasure resigned the remainder to his Lordship, who she was happy to find so worthy of filling the place of his ancestors. She at the same time acquainted him with her motives for concealing her intentions in his favor, and that, had she seen him addicted to any irregularities, she would not have assigned over the property so soon to him – as the law of this country does not interfere like that of France, where, if a person, before he attains the age of twenty-five, wastes his fortune by anticipation, or other means, and is in a fair way of ruining himself, and, perhaps, his family; the government interposes: guardians of his estate are appointed, and his person may be detained in custody till he arrives at that age; but *there* the jurisdiction stops. The acknowledgments of Lord Munster are easier to be conceived, than expressed – he concluded by saying, 'he hoped Lady Frances would always consider Munster-house as still her own, and make it her principle residence!' She smiled, and looking to Lord Darnley, said, 'Having my lord performed my duty to this family; it is now in my power to make myself happy by conforming to your wishes – Sixteen years ago, I had singly an engagement to fulfil; but I have now a breach of it to repair.' Lord Darnley's joy may easily be supposed great on this occasion, who had maintained for Lady Frances, for so long a time, an uninterrupted attachment. – They were married a few days afterwards. Never did Phœbus gild a more auspicious day; never did Cupid inspire two lovers with a higher sense of each other's merit; and never did Hymen light his torch with a greater complacency, than to reward that constancy which remained invincible in Lord Darnley, without even being supported by hope.

The part Lady Darnley performed would have been difficult for another; but the club which a man of ordinary size could but lift, was but a walking-stick to Hercules.

No one enjoyed this wedding more than Mrs Dorothea Bingley. A sixteen years courtship corresponded entirely with her ideas of the right and fitness of things. She harangued her niece and Lady Eliza on this subject, telling them that Lady Darnley is the only woman she knows in this degenerate age, that has acted up to the propriety of the ancients – that she respected the sublimity of her ideas. She was very desirous of her niece's marrying a Mr Bennet, because he made love in heroics, was inebriated in his science, and thought all the world considered him as a Phoenix of wit. Miss Bingley would often reason with her aunt on this subject? 'Of what use in the world (said she) is an erudition so savage, and so full of presumption?'

> One moral, or a mere well-natur'd deed,
> Does all desert in sciences exceed.'
>   SHEFFIELD

But Mrs Dorothea always insisted that he was a classical scholar, and a fine gentleman! The niece declared he was a Pagan, and ought to have lived two centuries ago, as he spoke a language she did not understand! 'He may be learned (said she) but he has no passion!'

'No passion (replied Mrs Dorothea) how comes he then to write such fine letters?'

'The fine letters (replied Miss Bingley) show memory and fancy, but no sensations of *the heart!* lovers who make use of extravagant tropes are reduced to that expedient, to supply the defect of passion by the deceitful counterfeit of hyperbolical language. The passions of *the heart* depend not on the deductions of *the understanding* – but it was necessary he should have a *Corinna*, because Ovid had *one*; and he makes me inconstant, although I never gave him any encouragement, because Gallus's favourite run away with a soldier. He seems to be intimately acquainted with the history of Cupid and Venus, but knows nothing *of love*: and would be sooner applauded for writing a good elegy, than have his mistress smile on him.'

Mrs Dorothea told her, that she was exceedingly perverse, but she would give her leave *to talk*, as she had the power *to do*.

Miss Bingley said, 'Since Mr Bennet was so much in her good graces, she made no doubt but he would pay her his homage, on the smallest hint, would transfer his affections – as the foundation of his passion was *the same* for *both*, built on that of her *mansion*, would *grow* with her *trees* and *increase* with her *estate* —— Increase, you know, my dear aunt, is the end of marriage; and your fortune is better than Medea's charm, for that only made an old man young again; but your riches will make a young man enamoured of an old woman! He will swear you are not only wiser than Minerva, but fairer than the Paphian queen! Though you are old, your trees are green; and though you have lost the roses in your cheeks, there are great plenty of them on your pleasure-grounds.'

Mrs Dorothea with great good-humour laughed at her niece's sallies, saying, 'You remember what Martial says;

> 'Fain would kind Paula wed me if she could:
> I won't, she's old; if older yet, I would.'

'But seriously, niece (said she) you will never make a choice that I shall so much approve of – he has so much wit.'

Miss Bingley replied, that all the credit he has for wit is owing to the gratification he gives to others ill-nature: and said she would be very happy to accommodate herself to her aunt's wishes; but was not upon such a religious strain, and so desirous of canonization hereafter (if sufferings can make a saint) as to marry a man of his character, that she might have her moritifications and punishments in this life: but at the same time would faithfully promise never to marry any man she disapproved of.

There were great rejoicings for some weeks at Munster-house:— at which time Lord and Lady Darnley set out for their estate in Dorsetshire, and Lady Eliza accompanied Lord Munster to London. As a correspondence commenced at this period between the parties I have already introduced to the reader, the sequel of this history will appear from their letters. I shall only observe, that Lord Munster's figure was remarkably agreeable, his address engaging; he first attracted, and then commanded the admiration of all who knew him. On the slightest acquaintance with him, a most exact regard to all the proprieties and decencies of life were observable in his conduct; and such an evident desire to oblige, and to make all about him easy, as became a good mind and a liberal education. An agreeable chearfulness made his conversation as lively and agreeable as it was useful and instructing. But the discerning eye of friendship could discover that he was not happy, and that delicacy to the feelings of his friends restrained him from giving way to an uneasiness, which it was too apparent he laboured under. His general behaviour bore the genuine stamp of true politeness, the result of an overflowing humanity and benevolence of heart. Such qualities very justly and forcibly recommend, lying obvious to almost every observer; but to the more discerning, a nearer view of him quickly discovered endowments far above the common standard. He had, in truth, endowments of mind to have honored any station.

As Lady Darnley's breast glowed with that exalted fervent charity which embraces the wide extended interests of men, of communities, of the species itself; it is easy to conceive how her heart exulted at finding her nephew so deserving of all she had done for him. But though she felt the greatest satisfaction at his being so conformable to her wishes, and his fortune so adequate to his beneficence; the same sensibility rendered her wretched for the evident melancholy in which he was plunged. Her social affections ever awake, even on those whose objects lie beyond the nearer ties of nature, on many occasions gave her most painful sympathetic feelings; so deeply was she interested in the fortunes of all with whom she had any connection. How then must she mourn to observe, that, notwithstanding the possession of every advantage of person and wealth, her nephew was miserable! – If men would but consider how many things there are that riches cannot buy, they would not be so fond of them – for all the outward advantages Lord Munster had, were, to a man in his situation of mind, *landscapes* before a *blind man*, or *music* to one that *is deaf.*

Delicacy kept Lady Darnley from interrogating her nephew on the subject of his grief; sensible that the remotest desire *from her*, must amount to a command *to him.* She only, at parting, insinuated the happiness it would afford her to see him ally himself suitably to some lady of merit: and, as Lady Eliza was to accompany him to town, requested him to moderate her liveliness, and to be a careful observer of her conduct.

'I never see (said she) a single man, who hath passed middle age in celibacy, where no particular security arises from his profession or character; but I think I see an unsafe subject, and a very dangerous instrument for any mischief that his *own* parts may *inspire*, or *other men's* may *prompt him* to: As to other achievements of virtue, a distinction *ought*, I think, to be *made*; because, in common acceptation, there is a variety of things which pass under that name, and are generally applauded, which, properly estimated, would not *deserve it.* A regard to posterity hath carried arms, arts, and literature, further than any other motive ever did or could. Who is so likely to be influenced by this regard as they who are to leave behind them the darling pledges of their affection, in whom they hope to have their names continued, and all the fruits of their study, toil, and exploits, abiding and permanent?' Lord Munster assured the Countess, that he would ever think it his glory to conform to her wishes in ever respect.

END OF THE FIRST VOLUME

VOLUME II

SOON after Lord Munster's arrival in London, he wrote Lady Darnley the following letter.

From the Earl of Munster to the
Countess of Darnley.

'My Dear Aunt,

Over powered as I am with a weight of obligations, I should think myself highly wanting to my own feelings, were I in any one instance in my future life to leave you dubious of my gratitude, or the earnest desire I have of conforming to your wishes.

You have, my dear Madam, expressed your desire I should marry; but that, my dear aunt, is impossible at present. But I revere that state: men who laugh at a serious engagement, have never known the allurements of modesty when blended with affability; nor felt the power of beauty, when innocence has increased its force. This has been my case, and my heart is already a prey to a hopeless passion. But it is necessary to carry you back some years, in order to give a recital of its commencement.

The amiable character of Mr Vanhagen, my landlord at Rotterdam, you are already acquainted with: his humanity and benevolence inspired me with the greatest respect. The advantages his countrymen have over us, are their industry, vigilance, and wariness: But they in general exert them to excess, by which means they turn their virtues into vices. Their industry becomes rapine, their vigilance fraud, their wariness cunning. But my worthy landlord possessed all the virtues.

He had in the early part of his life resided much at Venice, and brought from thence the economy and frugality which distinguish them in their private families, their temperance, their inviolable secrecy of public and private affairs, and a certain steadiness and serenity to which the English are supposed to be utter strangers. His long residence there, made him well known to the duchess de Salis, whose distant relation he had married.

This lady had resided some years at Rotterdam with her family. She was only daughter to the Count de Trevier, was heiress to a large fortune, and possessed exquisite beauty, good-sense, and every accomplishment that was likely to preserve and to improve the authority beauty gives to make it *indefectible* and *interminable*. But the duke, her husband, unfortunately was soon satiated with the regularity of her virtues: His affections could not long be preserved by a woman of her amiable undisguised character. When custom had taken off the edge from his passion, he endeavoured to rouse his torpid mind by a change of object. That vivacity which the tender passions impart to pleasure, was a powerful incentive for him to indulge them. His heart found fresh delight in gallantry, to which he was naturally prone: a dangerous delight, which, habituating the mind to the most lively transports, gives it a distaste to all moderate and temperate enjoyments: from thence forward the innocent and tranquil joys which nature offers, lose all their relish. His sophisticated mind made him blind to the merit of his wife, who loved him tenderly. – She felt most severely his neglect, and contracted insensibly a settled melancholy, which served the more effectually to alienate his affections from her. She became miserable:– and no temper can be so invincibly good as to hold out against the siege of constant slights and neglects. Misfortunes she had strength of mind to support, and death she could have encountered with greater resolution than the displeasure and peevishness of the man she loved. Wherever there is love, there is a degree of fear – we are naturally afraid of offending, or of doing any thing which may lessen us in the esteem of an object that is dear to us: and if we are conscious of any act by which we may have incurred displeasure, we are impatient and miserable, till, by intreaties and tokens of submission, we have expiated the offence and are restored to favor.

By the duchess's earnest solicitude to please, she destroyed her own purpose, and her obedience, like water flung upon a raging fire, only inflamed her husband's follies; and therefore, when he was in an ill humour, the duke vented his range on her. He did not care *how* often *he quarrelled* with, or, to speak more properly, how often he *insulted* her; for that could not be called a quarrel wherein she acted no part but *that of suffering*. But though his displeasure was grievous to her, yet she could bear it better than his indifference — for resentment argues some degree of regard. But whilst she was breaking her heart for him, he passed his time in gallantry – though his affections were always the satire of a woman's virtue – the ruin of a woman's reputation.

A favourite mistress, by pursuing a different plan from that of the duchess, secured his affections. She kept alive his ardour by her caprices. *Affectation* always exceeds the *reality*. But is not the extravagance of some men's fancy to be pitied, who lodge all their passions in a mistress, a dog, or a horse, which but in general do them no service but what they are prompted to through necessity or instinct? Art and cunning are *unknown* to a woman of virtue, whose conduct is determined by her principles, whose anxiety alone is excited by affection.

After five years, in which the duchess had a son and a daughter, and in which she had experienced many of the *vexations*, but few of the *satisfactions* of a married state; the duke left her, and resided entirely in Paris with his mistress. She retired to the country, to a family-seat of her father's, and devoted her time entirely to the education of her children, and that of a young lady (of great beauty and fortune) whose mother with her last breath bequeathed to her care.

She from time to time wrote the duke letters, expressing great resignation, and such a tenderness for him as she thought might have power to touch his heart. "I am obedient to your wishes," said she, "I will not urge, with one unwelcome word, this unkindness – I'll conceal it – If your heart has made a choice more worthy, I forgive it – pursue your pleasures – drive without a rein your passions – I am the mistress of my own mind, that shall not mutiny – If I retrieve you, I shall be thankful – If not, you *are* and must be still *my lord*."

To letters such as these she never received any answer! as the charms of a woman's eloquence never have any force, when those of her person are expired (in the eyes of her lover I mean): it might be perhaps as easy to persuade a man to dance, who had lost the use of his limbs.

I shall pass over the first ten years of her retirement, as they furnish nothing more than the unwearied attentions she took in employing every means for the instruction of her son, daughter, and ward. I shall only observe, that the regularity of her conduct gained her the esteem of every one. She was a friend to virtue under any denomination, and an enemy to vice under any colour. She established an institution for the provision of the infirm and destitute. This was constructed on that wise and excellent plan, that excludes the undeserving from participating in the charity, and extends only to those who, from their real necessities, are proper objects of benevolence. – At that period she was advised to take her son to the capital. But she wisely considered that the education which commonly attends high birth or great fortune, very often corrupts or sophisticates nature; whilst in those of the middle state she remains unmixed and unaltered. I have somewhere read; *Jamais les grandes passions et les grandes vertus ne sont nées, & ne se sont nourriès que dans le silence & la retrait. L'homme en societé perd tous ses traits distinctifs: ce ne'est plus qu' une froide copie de ce qui l'environne. Voilà pour quelle raison on nous accuse de manquer de caractere: nous ne vivons pas assez avec nous-mémes, & nous empruntons trop des autres.*

The duchess procured for her son's tutor, a very respectable man, who was at the utmost pains in forming his morals, and improving his understanding; while so many of the degenerate nobility in great cities are trifling away their time and their fortunes, in idle dissipations, in sensual enjoyments, or irrational diversions, and making mere amusement the great business of their lives. Happiness and merit are the result, not so much of truth and knowledge, as of attaining integrity and moderation. Many ridiculed the duchess's plan of education, of debarring herself from those pleasures and enjoyments her youth, rank, and beauty so well intitled her to: But she often observed it would be the height of imbecility to judge of her felicity by the imagination of others; considering nothing under the title of happiness, but what she wished to be in the possession of, or what was the result of her own voluntary choice. Women of the world counteract their intention, in so assiduously courting pleasure, as it only makes it fly further from them. They will not understand, that pleasure is to be purchased, and that industry is the price of it; to reject the one, is to renounce the other. They are to learn that pleasure, which they idolize, must now and then be *quitted* in order to be *regained*. They have tried in vain to perpetuate it, by attempting variety and refinement. Their fertile invention has multiplied the objects of amusement, and created new ones every day, without making any real acquisition. All these fantastic pleasures, which are founded on variety, make no lasting impressions on the mind; they only serve to prove the impossibility of permanent happiness, of which some women entertain *chimerical expectations*: but the duchess was too rational to make amusement her principal object. A woman that is hurried away by a fondness for it, is, generally speaking, a very useless member of the community: A party of pleasure will make her forget every connection: and she is often sick without knowing *where* her complaint *lies*, because she has nothing *to do*, and is tired of being *well*.

The duchess had loved her husband passionately. If any person had a desire of ingratiating themselves with her, they had only to begin by him: To praise, to please, or admire him, opened to them a reception in her heart. But our best virtues, when pushed to a certain degree, are on the point of becoming vices: She soon found she was to blame, in dedicating herself to fondly even to this beloved object. She exhausted her whole sensibility on him, and in proportion to the strength of her attachment, was the mortification she endured in being abandoned by him. But had not even this been her fate, the extravagant excesses of passion are but too generally followed by an intolerable langour. The woman who wishes to preserve her husband's affection, should be careful to conceal from him the extent of *hers*: there should be always something left for him to expect. Fancy governs mankind: and when the imagination is cloyed, reason is a slave to caprice.

Women do not want judgment to determine, penetration to foresee, nor resolution to execute; and Providence has not given them beauty to create love, without understanding to preserve it. The pleasures of which they are susceptible, are proportioned to the capacity and just extent of their feelings. They are not made for those raptures which transport them beyond themselves: these are a kind of convulsions, which can never last. But there are infinite numbers of pleasures, which, though they make slighter impressions, are nevertheless more valuable. These are renewed every day under different forms, and instead of excluding each other, unite together in happy concert, producing that temperate glow of mind which preserves it vigorous, and keeps it in a delightful equanimity. How much are those of the fair-sex to be pitied who are insensible to such attainments, and who look upon life as gloomy, which is exempt from the agitation of unruly passions! As such prepossessions deprive them of pleasures which are much preferable to those which arise from dangerous attachments, the duchess knew how to make choice of her amusements, and *improved* her *understanding* at the same time that she *gratified* her *feelings*. Life to those who know how to make a proper use of it, is strewed with delights of every kind, which, in their turn, flatter the senses and the mind; but the latter is never so agreeably engaged as in the conversation of intelligent persons, who are capable of conveying both instruction and entertainment. The duchess preferred the conversation of *such*, to *men of the world*; being sensible she had every thing *to gain* on *one side*, and every thing *to lose* on *the other*.

The Baron de Luce resided in the same part of the country. He was a man of great gallantry, wit, and humour. He judged it impossible that a woman in the bloom of beauty, possessed of the united advantages resulting from rank, riches, and youth, should retire to an obscure part of the world, and sequester herself from (what he judged) the pleasures of life, without being *compelled* by her husband or *prompted* by some secret inclination which she wished to conceal. Determined to unravel this mystery, and to amuse himself during the time he staid in the neighbourhood, he tried to insinuate himself into her good opinion – but without giving any offence she avoided entering into his plans. He still persisted in his intentions, judging, as he wrote well, the duchess would be glad to enter into a correspondence; but he found nothing in the reception she gave him that was for his purpose, *to embellish the history of his amours.* But what he undertook at first from vanity, became at last sufficient punishment for him. The more he saw of her conduct the more his respect increased, but which instead of making him relinquish his *intentions* (from a conviction of the inefficacy of the pursuit) made him persist *in them*, as he *then felt* the passion which at *first he feigned.*

The duchess knew the predicament on which she stood; but as *the hatred* of men of a certain character is *less* pernicious than *their love*, she gave orders never to admit him into her presence. The good or bad reputation of women depends not so much upon the propriety of their own conduct, as it does upon a lucky or unlucky combination of circumstances in certain situations. Some men calumniate them for no other reason, but because they are in love with them. They revenge themselves upon them for the want of that merit which renders them despicable in their eyes. This was the case with the Baron; he insinuated there were reasons which he knew that rendered it highly proper for the duchess to live in the manner *she did*, speaking in a *style* which conveyed more than met the ear! The people he addressed greedily listened to what seemed to bring the duchess more on a footing with themselves; a thousand stories were circulated to her prejudice (though innocence itself): Thus if there be but the least foundation for flander, some people believe themselves fully authorized to publish whatever malice *dares invent.* But there are no enemies more dangerous to the reputation of women, than lovers that cannot gain the reciprocal affection of their mistresses. These reports were confirmed from another cause — A lady of fortune in the neighbourhood became much attached to a man who resided with the duchess as her son's tutor; he was ingenuous, sensible, and much respected. She offered him her hand, and as she possessed a handsome fortune could not conceive how he could decline that happiness. As he was constantly at home, agreeable to the stories that had been circulated, she concluded at once (and then affirmed) he was a favourite of the duchess.

Self-love is of the nature of the polypus; though you sever her branches or arms, and even divide her trunk, yet she finds means to reproduce herself. In consequence of the information the duke received from this lady, who wrote to him in the character of an anonymous friend, he left Paris and his mistress abruptly; and, to the great surprise of his wife, came to – . He accosted her in a distant, but respectful manner. – Nothing gives so sharp a point to one's aversion as good-breeding – The duchess, unconscious of having given him any occasion of offence, was highly delighted at his return, flattering herself with a return of his affection. And as she considered him the aggressor, received him graciously, insisting that no mention should be made of past transactions; assuring him that she still retained the same love for him, and as she regarded him as the first of human beings, had perhaps been too sanguine in expecting his constancy, as so many temptations must occur from his superiority to the rest of mankind. She thought he was but too amiable – that his very *vices* had charms beyond other mens *virtues*. Adding that (grievous as his neglect had been to her) yet she had never done anything that could reflect upon his honor! He heard her in a sullen humour; his inclinations *were revived* by remarking, that time, instead of *diminishing*, had *added to her charms*: this increased his resentment, and he answered, that the worst a bad woman can do, is to make herself ridiculous; it is on herself only that she can entail infamy — but men of honor have a degree of it to maintain, superior to that which is in a woman's keeping. Had she had a mind to retaliate, she might easily have said, that a man of honor and virtue which, in themselves indeed, are always inseparably connected, are but too often separated in the absurd and extravagant opinions of mankind. For what a strange perversion of reason is it, to call a person a man of honor who has scarcely a grain of virtue! She only observed, we are indeed civilized into brutes; and a false idea of honor has almost reduced us into Hob's first state of nature, by making us barbarous. Honor now is no more than an imaginary being, worshipped by men of *the world*, to which they frequently offer human sacrifices. He told her she needed not *be troubled for her minion*: and retiring to rest, left her quite at a loss to account for his conduct.

It is not sufficient we know our own innocence; it is necessary, for a woman's happiness, not to be suspected.

For unfortunately after she has been once censured (however falsely) she must expect the envenomed shafts of malice ever ready to be let fly at her, and that in the transaction of any affairs that will admit of two interpretations (to avoid the worst, and enjoy an unblemished reputation). It is not enough to govern herself with propriety, there must be nothing that will carry two interpretations in the *accidents of her life*: A woman must therefore be necessarily always guilty, when innocence has need of many justifications. Happy are those who are not exposed to such inconveniences!

The Duke most injudiciously next morning publicly dismissed the object of his jealousy, and, by his want of prudence, confirmed every thing that had been falsely alledged against his innocent wife, who continued ignorant of it for some months.

When acquainted with it — The less ground she saw for the reports against her honor, the more courage and greater resolution she had to condemn them. She thought herself unfortunate to have lost the merit of her innocence by scandalous reports which she thanked Heaven she had not incurred by her guilt: and was so far from slighting the probabilities that might confirm opinions founded against her, that she by no means thought herself in the same situation with others, who had never *been contemned*, and that consequently she was not at liberty to act on some occasions as *they might do*.

How many women *err* from the obstinacy of people in defaming them — they give up the point, despairing of success in conciliating the esteem of a world who never *retract censure* — It is not with detraction as it is with other things that displease by repetition: Stories that have been told a thousand times, are still new when revived to the prejudice of another. The duchess bore all these calumnies with patience, *which* was never yet a *solitary virtue*: like an angler she endeavoured to humour the duke's waywardness, flattering herself that her study to please would conquer his disagreeable temper; and that if she could not become a pleasing wife, she might at least be thought an agreeable companion, a serviceable friend. Hope was the only blessing left us, when Pandora's fatal box let out all the numberless evils which infest these sublunary regions. But she was at last obliged to resign all ideas of submitting longer to his caprices. He became jealous even of his menial servants; and she could speak to no man without incurring his suspicions; which produced to her the most mortifying scenes. Like that conqueror of China, who forced his subjects into a general revolt, because he wanted to oblige them to cut their hair and their nails, he reduced her to form the resolution of leaving him, because (as he represented it) *he had dismissed a servant*. But it was in reality his temper and abuse that occasioned it – and when she was under the necessity of taking that step, she rather let the world judge amiss of her, than justify herself at her husband's expense. No condescensions on *her* part could affect *him*, as daily experience convinced her, that from a consciousness of the part he *himself had acted*, he could never *love her*. Are there not many occasions in life in which it would be reasonable to say, *I conjure you to forget and forgive the injury you have done me?*

They at last parted amicably: she came to Rotterdam with her family, and there I contracted an intimacy with her son, who was an amiable young man about my own age. There I first beheld the lovely Adelaude, Countess de Sons, the duchess's ward: the first time I saw *her*, and the charming Julia, I know I had *a heart*; until then I was insensible – These young ladies were instructed in all the arts of Minerva; Julia was skilled in music; but the countess's voice was, accompanied with the lyre, more moving than that of Orpheus. Her hair hung waving in the wind without any ornament, which the duchess had taught her to despise: her motions were all perfectly easy, her smiles enchanting! Without dress she had beauty, unconscious of any, and thus were heightened all her charms.

The marquis enquired what I thought of his sister, and her fair friend? I answered, "They were charming," and asked if it was possible he had resisted the charms of the beautiful countess? He replied, "I will own to you, my dear friend, I have not:" Adelaude is formed for love; my heart is naturally susceptible; she has been my constant companion: he must be something more, or something less than a man (a god or a devil) who hath escaped, or who can resist love's empire. – The gods of the heathens could not; Jupiter, Mars, Mercury, Apollo, their amours are as famous as their names: so that sturdiness in human nature, where it is found, which can resist, argues plainly how much the devil is wrought up in the composition. But if my sensibility had not been so great, yet so many opportunities she has had to engage my affections, could not fail of rivetting me her's for ever," "You are beloved then" said I hastily. "Yes," replied he, "Adelaude calls me her dearest brother; but entertains no ideas beyond that relation; and I am fearful of letting her know the extent of my sentiments, lest it should render her constrained in her manner to me; and the charming *naiveté* of her behaviour forms the charms of my life! The marks of that innocent affection, which first attached me to her, have hitherto been looked upon as a childish play: and as no one has troubled their head about the consequences of it, I have taken care to profit by the liberty allowed me. — You make me no answer! – Wherefore this gloomy silence, your dejected air, and languishing looks?' I pretended an indisposition, and left him under the greatest oppressure of spirits; I loved, I adored the charming Countess! judge then of the horror of my situation. –

How many sacrifices could I not willingly have made to friendship! My passion I thought was indeed the only one I could not make: how was it possible I should? but convinced of the happiness of my rival, what did I not suffer? I saw a pair of happy lovers, suited to each other; I thought it would be safe to alienate her affections; and considered myself only in the light of a dependent on your bounty: in such a situation, had my friend been uninterested, could I hazard addressing a young lady of the countess's rank and fortune? I became melancholy and *distrait*. Many people, and particularly those who have no idea of that delicacy of passion peculiar to susceptible minds, looked on me as a particular kind of a young man. To please such persons, I must have devoted my time to them: you will easily conceive then, I could well enough bear the want of their good opinion. Such become the artificers of their own misfortunes, by the false idea they form of pleasure, and they philtre (if I may use the term) their own sorrows.

It was what is called pleasure, that sunk into ruin the ancient states of Greece; that destroyed the Romans, that overturns cities; that corrupts courts; that exhausts the fortunes of the great; that consumes youth; that has a retinue composed of satiety, indigence, sickness, and death. But *my passion*, as much as a *dislike* to their *manner of life*, secured me from *their dissipations*. The constant endeavours I used to suppress an inclination I could not overcome, had a fatal effect on my constitution – I was threatened with a consumption! – This I carefully concealed, lest your kindness should have urged my removal from a place, which I could not determine to quit: though I carefully avoided the sight of those who were interesting to me in it.

At this time the marquis received a peremptory command to rejoin his father. He came to me in the greatest distress: "How", said he, "can I resolve to leave the countess? – She is now beautiful as an angel, exclusive of her immense fortune; to remain single cannot possibly be long in her power, for her beauty must necessarily strike every eye, and charm every heart. But I will go and unburthen myself to my father; her riches and rank will insure his approbation. You, my friend, alone are acquainted with the secret of my heart. See the lovely Adelaude often; to you I confide the secrets of my soul. Farewel."

The marquis set out, and soon informed me that his father would not yet hear of his marriage, and had insisted on his immediately joining a regiment in which he had procured him a command: It was in time of war; his honor at stake, and love was subordinate to his glory. The susceptible mind is capable of enjoying a thousand exquisite delights to which those are strangers, whose pleasures are less refined; but what chagrin, what regret, what pain does not so delicate a passion bring on the heart that entertains it? *Quand on est né trop tendre, on ne doit pas aimer*, says some French author. But the sufferings of my friend could not equal mine; the object of my passion being daily before my eyes heightened my inquietude. The general characters of men, I am apt to believe, are determined by their natural constitutions, as their particular actions are by their immediate objects. The innocent marks of partiality she honored me with, made me in constant fears of acting dishonorably to the marquis. The duchess fell soon after into a languishing illness, which in a short time put a period to her life: The duke came, but *too late*, to receive her last breath. He at first appeared inconsolable for her death; but his grief insensibly decreased, and softened into that mournful and tender regard, which a sense of her merit, and his own unkindness to her, could not fail of exacting from him. Disgusted at an union, which had caused him (from his own errors) so much uneasiness, he formed a resolution carefully to avoid entering again into a similar engagement. But he saw every day before him the lovely Adelaude: he loved her; it was perhaps impossible for him to do otherwise. He declared his passion; but was rejected: The countess told him her affections were engaged! Next day I received the following letter.

From the Countess de Sons to the Earl of Munster.

My Lord,

I am well aware of the delicacy which prescribes certain observances to our sex. But there is no rule in life which must not vary with circumstances. Come to me this evening: Julia will be with me – Adieu.

ADELAUDE de SONS.

I went – Abashed at the step she had taken, the cheeks of the lovely Adelaude glowed with the most lovely red; her eyes sparkled with the brightest lustre; while the loves and graces hovered around her charming form, and fluttered on her breast – Love, almighty love, preceded her steps, when she approached me. Heavens! how quick my heart beat at that instant with pleasing hope! I endeavoured to speak to her, but hesitated and trembled. After a few moments' expressive silence, I desired to know what commands she meant to honor me with? She was greatly confused, but at length told me the dilemma she was in from the declaration of the duke's passion. To support my politics, I began and talked of my friend.

She told me that his partiality was no secret to her, although he had never disclosed it, but that she rejoiced at his absence, as it would enable him to triumph over a passion she could *not return*. Surprised at this declaration, I should have been wanting to myself not to improve it. But love only can give an idea of those pleasures we enjoyed in each other's company with reciprocal tenderness. But *it* affords few sweets that are not dashed with a mixture of bitterness. Happy moments! how soon ye fled! a sad remembrance only of that delightful interval left behind. Ah no, it is impossible I should ever forget that day in which she first confessed those sentiments for me my heart had long divined, the assurance of which, nevertheless, gave me inexpressible transport. But when I reflected on my friend, and that of my depressed circumstances, it gave a sudden check to my joy. My sighs, my tears, made known to her the distress of my heart! I could only utter the name of *my friend*, and wrung my hands in despair. She soothed my uneasiness. "This is the fatal stroke I feared" said the gentle Adelaude; "this is what my foreboding heart presaged. But your interest does not interfere with his, for whom I never experienced any thing more but that of a *sisterly affection*."

I then acquainted her with my dependent situation: that I should be hurt at allying her so unsuitably, though had I had the wealth of worlds it would have been hers. She told me her estate was sufficient to enrich me: that the duke talked of leaving Rotterdam; she dreaded being in the power of a man so impetuous, who would stick at nothing to gratify his passions; and that she would place herself under my protection. Infatuated I was, not to comply with her request! My friend's woes wounded me to the quick: false honor determined me to write and inform him of the state of the affair, previous to my taking advantage of her inclination for me. I wrote instantly to the marquis; but a few days after the duke set out for Italy with his family. The night before their departure I saw the countess. "Thou must go," said I, "and with thee all my joy, my happiness, my only hope – Go, and take with thee all my heart holds dear, all that is left for me is despair. Reason will resume its empire over love, and you will forget a poor unfortunate, who hath nothing to offer but the most pure and ardent affection; an affection in which consists all the happiness of his life."

"Ah, my lord," said she, "forbear to speak a language so injurious to your merit and my sentiments. Can I cease to love you? Can I forget you? No! whilst my heart beats it will be yours, and yours only – I will preserve myself for you, and nothing can ever make me forgetful of the engagements I have made with you."

The conflict of contending passions had tortured me so much, that I confess, I was rather relieved, when they set out, and when it was out of my power to have realized the charming scheme the countess had suggested to me. What forbearance did it not cost me? Nothing is more common than for men to declaim against those things which they are not in a capacity to enjoy: Diogenes said to Aristippus the courtier, as he passed him in his tub, "If you could content yourself, as I do, with *bread* and *garlic*, you would not be the *slave* of the King of Syracuse:" "Are you," replied Aristippus, "if you *knew* how to *live with princes*, you would not make such *bad cheer*."

Perhaps the circumstances of age, health, and fortune, vary the taste, and regulate the appetites of mankind more than reason and reflection.

But everything conspired to render the sacrifice I had made a *great one* to *friendship*. I soon received the following letter from Julia.

"My Lord,

The countess is so closely watched, that she cannot write. Would to God you had followed your inclinations! We are going to Sweden: follow us, if possible, and repair the error you have committed. I am fearful she will be constrained to choose another husband. Adieu.

JULIA de VILLEROI."

Upon the receipt of this letter I went to Sweden; but could hear no tidings of those I pursued. I became quite melancholy, and seldom went abroad, but could not refuse being introduced by the Baron de R——— to the Queen Dowager, who is an exalted character: she is sister to the reigning King of Prussia, is the avowed protectress of letters, and encourager of merit: and during her husband's life possessed an almost unlimited influence over affairs of state; but at present leads a more retired and secluded life. She is perfect mistress of Latin, as well as the modern languages.

The present King of Sweden at the age of twenty-six changed the form of government, without blood or difficulty. Sweden can boast of her two Gustavus's, the first and second; nor are her Christina, or her Charles, unknown to fame. In what country is not the name of Peter celebrated, the greatest legislator that modern times have seen? Hearing no tidings of the duke's family, I made out my northern tour. In Denmark the sun of genius has not yet blazed from a throne, and shed a temporary lustre on the surrounding darkness; if we except the celebrated Margaret de Waldemar, to whom history has given the epithet of the *Semiramis* of the north, who united under her reign all the kingdoms beneath the polar sky, Denmark, Norway, and Sweden. There are, however, two favourite monarchs of Danish story. The first of these was Christian IV, who was the opponent and competitor of Gustavus Adolphus, but with far inferior fame. The last was Frederic IV. This prince loved the arts, and made two visits to Italy, one previous to his ascending the throne, and one after it. During a carnival at Venice, he resided in that city, and in one evening is said to have won, at the card-table, a bank worth one hundred thousand pounds sterling, which he immediately presented to a noble Venetian lady, in whose house this happened, and whose whole fortunes were involved in this game of chance: All the company were in masque.

I cannot omit mentioning the literary merit of the ladies in

Denmark; which has already been taken notice of by Lord Molesworth, who says, that Tycho Brahe's sister, and especially Dorothea Engelerechtie, may contend with the famous poetesses of the ancients. The lady Brigetta Tot has translated Seneca the philosopher into the Danish tongue, with all the elegance any language is capable of, and has conspired with our ingenious countrywoman Miss Carter*, to shew that the most rugged philosophy of the stoics must submit, when the fair-sex is pleased to conquer. But I forget who I am writing to – Thanks to your extensive reading – I have nothing to tell you that has been written and published before. I shall only observe, that I met with many ingenious men abroad who held the English cheap. I can account for this in no other way, than that they form their judgment of us only by the *philosophical transactions*. Absorbed in deep melancholy, on account of my ignorance of the fate of Countess de Sons, I went little into company, but applied myself constantly to study: I amused myself in painting; the cataract of the river Dahl is the subject of one of my pieces. The tremendous roar of these cataracts, which, when close, is superior to the loudest thunder; the vapours which rise incessantly from them, and even obscure them from the eye in many parts; the agitation of the river below for several hundred yards before it resumes its former tranquillity; and the sides covered with tall firr; form one of the most picturesque and astonishing scenes to be beheld in nature's volume.

Wrapt up one day in the contemplation of this scene, Lord Ogilby whom I became acquainted with at Upsal, approached me under an apparent agitation of spirits. We lived much together, but I had observed him very absent, and missed him several evenings. My Lord, said he, near this place resides all that my soul holds dear: I am in love – in love, to a degree I never felt till now. I am myself astonished at it. But blame me not until you see the object of my affections. He said, that he had been charmed with a young woman's figure and beauty, and that she appeared to be possessed of the greatest modesty, prudence, and good humour. He finished his

* Miss Carter translated Epictetus.

panegyric with saying, *how happy will that man be who first inspires her gentle heart with love!*

I accompanied Lord Ogilby (who remained silent) for about a hundred yards, when we approached a cottage.

A window being opened, he said to me, There, my Lord, you can see her without being observed. I looked, and beheld a most exquisite Beauty. She was of a fair complexion, had fine full blue languishing eyes, which sparked through the long lashes of their beautiful lids, and expressed, with the most innocent simplicity, all that an insipid coquet attempts in vain. When she perceived we looked at her, it heightened the vermilion on her cheeks, through the consciousness that they betrayed the extreme sensibility of her heart; and if even the rest of her person had not been equally engaging, yet the bewitching sweetness of her countenance alone would have intitled her to be ranked among the first class of pleasing Beauties. — A beautiful boy of about two years of age, whose hair flowed in natural ringlets like her own, was playing beside her while she was making some artificial flowers. Her dress was a brown camblet jacket and petticoat clasped at the breast.

Upon perceiving us she arose, and received us with the greatest politeness – It was easy for us to conceive she had been accustomed to genteel life. She acquainted us that whatever honor we might do her in condescending to come into that poor cottage, yet she must for the future desire we would not repeat our visit. As it was entirely contrary to her plans, and to those views which determined her to retire to that place. There appeared in her a timid bashfulness; but as this seemed to proceed from the fear of *my friend*, who had been importunate lover, and was a proof of the purity of her heart instead of an awkwardness, it appeared a grace. Yes, I repeat it, this bashfulness appeared in her quite engaging; for as the shade in a beautiful picture, it served to set off the masterly strokes of the piece. Lord Ogilby assured her in my hearing, that he had no views but which were highly honourable, that if she would give him her hand he would make her his wife. "I am one of those, said he, who have ever despised the common prejudices of mankind, particularly in the affair of love. A fine person, a graceful carriage, an amiable disposition, are all the titles or wealth I should look for in a woman. You possess all these advantages, and to them add the greatest delicacy of sentiment — so many charms compensate for the want of those other qualifications the injustice of fortune has deprived you of." – "Hymen, my lord, answered she, can have no joys for me, and I am sure will never light his torch on my account; for I have fountains of tears which would soon extinguish it!" What was my surprise to discover this beautiful girl (for her age did not appear to exceed eighteen) so accomplished, that she could read the Iliad of Homer, the Georgics of Virgil, the inimitable Cervantes, and the plays of Terence, in the original languages, with great ease! She was a *Hebe*, with the head of a philosopher, the knowledge of a divine, accompanied with all the exterior accomplishments the most finished education could bestow. As we found her fond of reading, we carried her a book of periodical papers then just written at Vienna. The next time I saw her I inquired if she approved of it – she replied she was no judge; but that she apprehended humour in writing chiefly consists in an imitation of the foibles or absurdities of mankind; so our pleasure in this species of composition, arises from comparing the picture with the original in nature, which she had no opportunity of doing.

In the works of our own countrymen we have frequent opportunities of making this comparison, as the originals are generally before us: But when we read the productions of foreigners, as their portraits are copied from manners with which we are not sufficiently acquainted, they must often appear forced and unnatural. There is a cast of humour, as well as of manners, peculiar to each country; and this is what makes every nation give the preference to its own humorous subjects. Nor is this preference ill founded, since the several drawings are made from originals widely different from each other; and as in portrait-painting, the value of the picture is enhanced by our connections with the person who sat for it; so here we must approve those pieces the originals of which we are best acquainted with. The language of humour is also in every country different from that used upon common occasions, which makes foreign satire an exotic of too delicate a nature to bear transplanting.

I was not surprised at my friend's situation; nothing I *then* supposed could have secured my own heart from her attractions but its being pre-engaged. All the great heroes, the scripture worthies in particular, have had their *Delilah's*, to whose bewitching charms they have *one and all yielded*; reluctantly some, and fondly others; *these* proving their wisdom, and *those* their folly; since *there is no enchantment against beauty*, nor any thing it cannot enchant.

But notwithstanding my predilection in her favor, prudence suggested to me that my friend's passion might hurry him into an improper connection. I therefore inquired particularly concerning this lovely woman. I found she had resided there fifteen months, having brought with her a maid, and the child whom we had seen: that soon after her arrival she had disposed of some valuable effects; and that she had employed herself since that period in making artifical flowers, which her maid carried to — and disposed of them: that it was with great pleasure they observed she was now much more cheerful than she had been at first. That she was very regular in her conduct; never saw any person, nor went abroad but for divine service or a little air and exercise. This account served only to increase my friend's passion. He left nothing unsaid, nothing undone, to convince her of his sincerity; but she remained inexorable! We were there one day; when I took the liberty of remonstrating with her on this subject: She was affected, and said, "My lord, you distress me greatly; but at once to relieve myself *from your* friend's importunities, and to prove *to you* how unavailable *his* pursuit *is*, I must be reduced to the humiliating detail of *my sorrows*: then, pointing to the lovely boy, she added, that cherub calls me *mother*, although his cruel father has not given me the name *of wife*: let this, my lord, render you unsolicitous concerning me."

Lord Ogilby, though struck at the intelligence, assured her, that she was infinitely superior in his eyes to women of the world, who vainly flatter themselves, that, while they appear *not* to be conscious of their errors, mankind never discover *their follies!* that he respected her candour, he would be a father to her lovely boy, and, by his tender faithful attachment, atone for her former disappointment. She said every thing a sensible heart could feel on the sense she had of the honor he did in addressing her on such honorable terms, in the strange situation he found her in; but added, her heart might break, but that in breaking it must be the entire property of Sir Harry Bingley!

I am very sensible, my lords, continued Miss Harris, that the foibles of those to whom we are indebted for our existence, though open to the attack of all the world beside, ought to be sacred to us. But it is incumbent on me to paint my father's character, in order to inform you of the origin of my misfortunes. He was the younger son of a family of distinction, had received every advantage of education, and had travelled all over the world; which he himself said had divested him of many narrow prejudices! But this was not sufficient for him – he must triumph over reason and nature. He was too wise to adopt the opinions of his fore-fathers, yet at the same time too indolent to establish any of his own; and as he lived without system, he made present convenience the rule of his conduct. His virtues consequently were *accidental* – but his vices *habitual*. A clergyman that kept him company countenanced *his errors*, and confirmed *my belief*, that religious duties were only an *imposition on the vulgar*. I am sure, my lord, you must agree with me in thinking that *immorality* in a *clergyman* is as unpardonable as *cowardice* in a *soldier*. *One* flies from the foes of his *king* and *country*; the *other* justifies the *enemies of his God*. My father married a young lady of large fortune. She had received a very religious education, and had too much sensibility not to be exceedingly wounded at his infidelity. He told her it was very well she thought as *she did* – that all capacities cannot command a sufficient degree of attention to pursue the intricacies of philosophical speculation; neither if they could, are they endowed with proper powers of perception to discern and judge for themselves. As these must necessarily be governed by prejudices, if you remove them, you leave such weak objects without any principle *whatever*.

My mother answered, that the apostles were no *metaphysicians*: nor did their blessed master teach them any thing that should make them so. Wherefore she contented herself with their plain instructions, finding much more satisfaction from them than she did from any human writers, especially those who use so many and so nice distinctions, tending more to *puzzle* than *enlighten* the understanding, and having little effect upon the heart to make it better. It is to me, I own, (said she) no recommendation of any cause, that the abettors of it are obliged to have recourse to *abstruse terms*, and especially when they introduce such terms into any system that pretends to be Christian. I admire no scholastic phrases, or terms of art, when applied to a doctrine which is matter of revelation only; and wherein neither schools nor arts have any thing to say further, nor can say any thing more clearly or more certainly than what God hath said. I am far from commending any imposition upon men's judgment, or any dictating by one man what is to be believed by another! But here my father interrupted her; and, in a passion, made use of terms delicacy prevents a repetition of – adding, neither *man* nor *woman* should dictate or make a fool of him! That religion, etc. etc. varied in different countries, as he had often observed something in the climate, soil, or situation of *each*, which had great influence in establishing its particular mode of superstition. Thus in Syria they worship the sun, moon, and stars, as they live in a flat country, enjoying a constant serenity of sky; and the origin and progress of that error may be traced in a certain connection between those objects of worship considered physically, and their characters as divinities.

Thus the pomp and magnificence with which the sun is worshipped in Syria, said he, and the human victims sacrificed to him, seem altogether to mark an awful reverence, paid rather to his power than to his beneficence, in a country where the violence of his heat is destructive to vegetation, as it is in many other respects very troublesome to the inhabitants. Superstition, since the world began, has consisted of every particular, which either people's *fears* or their *follies*, either the *strength* of their *imagination*, or the *weakness* of their *judgment*, or the *design* and *artifice* of their *leaders*, taught them to *embrace*, in order to please any being, or order of beings, superior to themselves, whom they made the objects of their religious regards. My mother answered, that the unbeliever changes nothing of the design of God, when he dares to rise up against him – He ever enters into his plan, where the evil concurs with the good, for the harmony of *this* world, and the good of the *next*. I need not, my lords, tire you with an account of these particulars, further than to mark the difference of my parents characters – these arguments recurring often, in the end produced such contentions, that it impaired my mother's health – she died, and left me under the guidance of a father, *totally unfit* for that *important trust*. He endeavoured to impress me with his sentiments of religion, etc. If I imbibed his ideas, could I be blamed for it? Is it not injurious and ridiculous to censure others for thinking in the same manner we ourselves should have done under the same circumstances? For if we do not consult our reason (which in matters of religion is prohibited us) the capacity and credulity of individuals are different, in consequence of their diversity of temperament, education, and experience. And it would be still more absurd to reprobate the rest of mankind, for not believing what we ourselves do *not*, nor can be made *to believe*. But to return to my father: About a year after my mother's death, when I was only eight years old, he set out for Italy, and returned home inebriated with a love for antiquity – He could sit all day in contemplation of a statue without a nose, and doated on the decays with greater love than the self-loved Narcissus did on his beauty. Sir Harry Bingley did me the honor to address me; but my father, on his first proposal, would not hear of it; he wished me to marry a brother antiquarian, who was desirous, among other pieces of age and time, to have one young face be seen to call him father. My lover told him, he would pray to Heaven to have merit or deserve me – He returned, "When your prayer is answered, renew your suit; but if you stay till then, you must have spectacles to see her beauty with." Had Sir Harry appeared to him like a Sibyl's son, or with a face rugged as father Nilus is pictured on the hangings, it would have been otherwise. But the qualities, which recommended him *to me*, produced the contrary effect on *my father*,

Signor Crustino, whom he favored, had presented him with books, that he said were written before the Punic war; and some of Terence's hundred and fifty comedies that were lost in the Adriatic sea, when he returned from banishment. –

There were powerful indocuments – He commanded me to marry him: I expostulated, but without effect. Had Sir Harry Bingley been old in any thing, even in iniquity, I believe he would have shown him some respect. Had he not, said he, the indiscretion to betray weakness, even to myself? did not he mention that his *old* rents produced one thousand a year; but that he had made *new* leases, and doubled them; and by the sale of a gallery of pictures had paid his father's debts? O such preposterous folly! he values more his gold, than whatever Apelles or Phidias have invented! "What is more honorable than age?" said he: "Is not wisdom entailed on it? It takes the pre-eminence in everything: antiquities are the registers, the chronicles of the age, and speak the truth of history better than a hundred of your printed commentaries!" It was in vain I pleaded a contrary opinion; my tears had no power to mollify his stony heart. I was ordered to prepare for my wedding; which I was determined, at all events, should not take place. In the mean time Sir Harry Bingley's passion was increased by the difficulty of obtaining me, as the lovers of the fair Danäe desired her more when she was locked up in the brazen tower. He was importunate with me to elope: inclination pressed hard on one side, duty on the other; I was torn with contending passions: my distraction was increased by the preparations for the marriage feast. My father took his bill of fare out of Athenæus, and ordered the most surprizing dishes imaginable. But I was reprieved by a most extra-ordinary accident – He was possessed of a couple of old manuscripts, said to have been found in a wall, and stored up with the foundation: he supposed them the writing of some prophetess – They were, he said, of the old Roman binding: And though the characters were so imperfect, that time had eaten out the letters, and the dust made a parenthesis betwixt every syllable, yet he was inconsolable upon discovering he had lost them; and suspected his brother antiquary of the theft, *such* generally being very *adroit* on *pilfering* – Words arose on the subject; they parted in wrath; my father declaring the marriage should not be celebrated. Signor Crustino next day wrote a mollifying letter, intreating his acceptance of several other manuscripts, which he said were dug out of the ruins of Aquileia, after it was sacked by Attila,

King of the Hunns. – But he returned them with indignation, and took to his bed, where he remained nine months in a very lingering condition – then died – leaving me a prey to the oppressive insolence of proud prosperity. — It is that only which can inflict a wound on the ingenuous mind. – These are the stings of poverty! Misfortunes never create respect: dependence of course meets with many slights – On such occasions, some show their *malice*, and are witty on our *misfortunes*; others their judgment, by sage reflections on our conduct; but few their charity. – They alone have a right to censure, who have hearts to assist: the rest is cruelty, not justice*.

I found that my father's collection of curiosities, for which he had expended all his fortune, did no more than pay his debts. On this occasion all my acquaintances forsook me. A rich aunt was the only person who recollected such a being existed (my lover excepted). She afforded me help, but more as if she had been giving *alms* to a *stranger*, than *relief* to a relation. How few are acquainted with the art of conferring favors in that happy manner that doubles the value of the obligation! If in doing good, people consulted the circumstances and inclinations of those they oblige – if, instead of shocking their self-love, (inherent in us all) they knew how to take advantage of it, with as much address as the flatterer employs to gain his ends, the empire of morality would long ago have extended its bounds, and the numbers of its adherents would have greatly increased. – This is the more easily done, as the *distressed* think any mark of attention shown them by the *wealthy, a real favor* – But *neglect* in general is the *portion* of the *necessitous* – and *outrage alone* employed to recover *the guilty*.

Lord Ogilby could not help here, with some warmth, asking where Sir Harry Bingley was all this time. Miss Harris bowed, and resumed her story. "Alas!" said she, "the Marquis of M——— his uncle, on whom he had considerable expectations, insisted on his marrying Lady Ann

---

* Francis the First of France, who had heavily taxed his subjects, when told the people made very free with his character in their songs, answered, 'It would be very hard if they were not allowed *to sing for their money.'*

Frivolité – and though he absolutely declined this overture, he thought in prudence, he ought to defer for some time entering into another engagement until he could bring his uncle to hearken to it."

My necessities increasing, relying entirely on the honor of my lover, I permitted him to conduct me to a seat he had in a remote part of the country – It was a frightful dismal house surrounded with yews and willows, whose different forms recalled to my ideas Ovid's Metamorphoses, and made me sometimes ready to bemoan the fate of unhappy lovers converted into evergreens by the supposed enchantress of this dreary mansion. The house had been long uninhabited: by the blackness of the walls, the circular fires, vast cauldrons, yawning mouths of ovens and furnaces, one would conclude, it was either the forge of Vulcan, the cave of Polypheme, or the temple of Moloch. The hangings of the apartments were indeed the finest in the world; that is to say, which Arachne spins from her own bowels. But the affection, the tender respectful behaviour of my lover was *everything to me*. He said he made no doubt but the marquis, when convinced of my merit, would approve of his passion! Unwilling to see him continue in so delusive an error, I told him there was little probability of reviving the golden age in his family; or, hoping that the benevolence of his own heart would become epidemical, was an illusion! that relations or parents saw things in a very different light from their children; as the sentiment of the former arose from cool reflection, and as those of the latter commonly resulted from the caprice of an irregular imagination, or the violence of an impetuous passion, which prompted them to act sometimes in direct opposition to the salutary advice of their best friends. – He replied, that granting that were even the case – the Marquis of M——— could not live for ever – but that no power on earth could induce him to sacrifice his happiness; that he had a *competent*, though not *great* estate of his own – and would marry me directly, if I chose it, or would take the most solemn oath imaginable, to do it as soon as circumstances rendered it prudent with safety. I consequently rejected agreeing to his proposal: I could not bear the idea of my lover's running the risk of losing a family inheritance on my account; though a possibility of possession altering his sentiments, never entered into my imagination. We remained three months together, the happiest time of my life: Happy moments, how soon you fled, never, never to return!

Miss Harris here blushed and stopped; we encouraged her to proceed. With some hesitation, she added, At that time my lover's importunity prevailed; I resigned myself to his wishes. I had his solemn promise he would ratify our engagement at the altar; and my father had instilled notions into me of marriage being only a civil institution: he had often said, that the marriages among the Israelites were not attended with any religious ceremonies, except the prayers of the father of the family, and the standers by, to beg the blessing of God. We have examples of it in the marriage of Rebecca with Isaac, of Ruth with Boaz. We do not read that God acted the part of a priest to join Adam and Eve together, only that of a father to the young woman, in giving her away — *For he brought her to the man*: We do not see, he used to say, that there were any sacrifices offered upon the occasion; that they went to the temple, or sent to the priests. So that it was no more than a civil contract. I also knew the present custom in Sicily and in Holland. Thus I justified myself *to myself*, though not effectually; but I was willing then *to believe* what *I wished*; as no inconvenience *to myself* could equally affect me in its consequences, as my lover losing his fortune on *my account*, which made me decline marrying him at that time. And I firmly relied on his honor, whom from that time I considered, and shall do, as my husband. With this difference – if a woman survives her husband, after some time set apart for decency, there are many circumstances may combine to render a second attachment eligible. But one who like me has evinced a weakness must be more exemplary in every other part of her character, and more tenacious in her conduct, least the *particular affection* which occasioned *her error*, should be imputed to her as a *depravity*. The event will prove, how requisite it is, for the good of society, that certain rules should be established, the infringers of which ought to suffer, for the good of the community.

The effect of our passion was soon evident in my person — but sorry I am to relate, grieved to repeat it — he left me; and at a time when I expected every minute to become a mother; without affording me one single line to *comfort* or *relieve* my mind from a state of distraction, little short of madness. I was at last told he had been obliged to set out on confidential business to the continent! Alas, in what way did I lose his confidence? His *glory* was dearer to me than my *own life*; and had he told me of the circumstances, I should have *urged* his *departure*, instead of wishing to *protract* his stay.

I was in despair for his unkindness! Had my steps been strewed with flowers, had I been possessed of every outward accommodation wealth could bestow, alas, how unavailing would all these advantages have been to me! but in my situation, oppressed, afflicted, and surrounded with mortifications, ignorant even of the means of my future support, and that of his child, how dreadfully were my woes increased! This mark of his inattention redoubled my grief. An assortment of flowers, plants, etc. arrived after his departure, which only served to remind me of the happiness I had proposed myself from their cultivation in his company: but I could not live by their scent, like a Dutch damsel, nor was I descended of Cameleons that could be kept with air. In my despair I refused all kind of nourishment; but a worthy girl who lived with me, recovered me from this *reverie*. If you are resolved, madam, (said she) never to eat a morsel more during your existence, your behaviour at present is very consistent; but if you design ever to do so, believe me that this is the best time you can possibly do so for yourself, exclusive of your child, who must suffer with you. The last argument was a prevailing one – I enquired for food, and eat greedily.

I was soon afterwards delivered of a lovely boy – I took him in my arms – each feature depicted his beloved, though cruel father! He has since been my only solace, comfort, and happiness – were I hunted out of society, and were I to meet with every species of abuse on *his account*, he would be infinitely more interesting to me than all that the world could confer upon me.

After two months, during which time I flattered myself I should hear from Sir Harry, though my hopes proved too sanguine, I removed from his house – I cared not where I went, if distant from a place he could discover me in, at a time when his capricious passion might bring him back to me. Many unfortunate women, in such a situation, give themselves up (as Ariadne did) to Bacchus, from the day they are deserted — But a superior education taught me better. My maid's brother was a captain of a ship; I agreed with him to bring us to this place. My child justified my keeping a few valuable trinkets Sir Harry had given me, which I should otherwise have returned – I set out, and, philsopher-like, carried all my possessions about me. These trinkets, and industry, have hitherto supported us – I revere virtue, though I have unhappily swerved from the established rules of virtue *in my country* — but I have the same warm affection for virtuous people, the same tenderness for the unhappy, and the same regard for those whom prosperity hath not blinded!

Lord Ogilby replied, Sir Harry Bingley must have been nursed among rocks, and suckled by tigers, to have used you thus! But you, even now, would prefer being the object of his licentious passion, rather than to become my virtuous wife! Miss Harris bowed, and replied, I flattered myself, my lord, that I had, though not without great confusion to myself, made you acquainted with my character – I therefore am highly superior to the inference you have indelicately made. I shall owe my future innocence to the sense I have of my lover's perfidy; as the sore wound the viper gives, the viper best cures. But my unfortunate circumstances exclude my ever thinking of any other of the sex: All the rest of mankind *are*, and must remain to me *a distinct species*. I would much rather die a thousand deaths, than that my heart should have once conceived such a thought! I have imprinted him in my heart in such deep characters, that nothing can rase it out, unless it rub my heart out. Although he has left me to be for ever miserable — may he be blessed – and may the fair-one whom he selects to be his happy, happy wife, love him the hundredth part I did! In this cottage will I remain! here dedicate my life to industry, to procure for the child of the man I love, the means of food and education: and when the great God calls upon me to offer up an account of all my deeds, I *cannot, do not* believe, I shall be found very defective in what his justice will exact from me. Though I lament the error I fell into, and am now convinced that we can have no distinct notions of human happiness, without the previous knowledge of the human constitution, of all its active and perceptive powers, and their natural objects: therefore the most natural method of proceeding in the science of morals, is to begin with inquiring into our several natural determinations, and the objects from whence our happiness can arise. — This, my lord, I have carefully done – my resolution is consequently fixed. Lord Ogilby again said, Madam, let me still intreat you to consider — If you have any hopes of his return, of all old debts, love, when it comes to be so, is paid the most unwillingly; and all you get by your constancy, is the loss of that beauty for *one lover*, which independent of my proposal to you, would procure you the vows, sacrifice, and service, of *a thousand!* She renewed her thanks for his lordship's good opinion; added, she entertained no hopes such as he had suggested, and must only beg leave to add, before she concluded, after entreating we would conceal his name, that it was not only a partiality for his person, but admiration of his character, that must bind her for ever his.

Lord Ogilby consigned a sum of money with her maid, that in case indisposition should interfere with her plans, she should still encounter no inconveniences.

I should not, my dear Aunt, have detained you so long with this story, did I not know your friendship to Sir Harry Bingley — I founded his sentiments, he is still fondly attached to this lovely woman — Honor, and a responsible situation, obliged him to leave her at the time, and his letters miscarried by the sudden death of a friend he entrusted them to. No part of my life, said he, can I recollect with so much satisfaction, as that which I spent with my lovely wife, for *such* I shall ever consider her. I reflect on the supposed injuries she thinks she has received from me, and I lament I know not *where she is* to make her every reparation in my power. Immediately on my arrival, I went to the place where I had left her — but no trace remained; she was fled, and had carried along with her the fruit of our affection. I have been fatigued with inquiries to no purpose – and conclude her dead; perhaps with grief for my supposed ingratitude.

Without letting Sir Harry know I was acquainted with his story, I discovered every thing from him I wished; and had the pleasure of hearing of his present independent fortunes, which put it in his power to realize the truth of his professions to Miss Harris. I sent off a courier to her – she is now on her return to England.

But to return to my own affairs – I went to Italy, but could hear no tidings of the Duke de Salis; was only informed, that his son, after some irregularities inherent in youth, had made a very good figure in the army, but for some time past had not been heard of — Nor was it known to what place the duke had retired. To amuse my chagrin, I went one evening to masquerade at Venice, in the time of the carnival, and fell in chat with a very agreeable young gentleman and his sister. They politely hoped our acquaintance would not cease at the end of the ball, and solicited a continuance of it – with this I very cheerfully complied. I went – and am mortified to betray my weakness to you; but truth obliges me to confess, that notwithstanding the pre-engagement of my heart for the Countess de Sons, yet I could not resist the attractions of Mademoiselle de Querci: my passion for her commenced the first moment I saw her; and her charming behaviour hourly increased it. She was majestic in her appearance; and in her were combined all the qualities that can make desirable the woman I adore.

The more I saw her, the more was her empire confirmed over me; but still dubious of the Countess's fate, and conscious of my pre-engagement, honor kept me silent. I had every reason to flatter myself my address would have been acceptable, but my passion was subordinate to that sense of honor my former obligations subjected me to. It is hard to account for the motions of the human heart, or trace the little springs that give rise to its affections — numberless latent accidents contribute to raise or allay them, without our being sensible of their secret influence. Thus situated, I came to England at your request. The uncertainty of the Countess's fate renders me wretched, while, to confess the truth, Mademoiselle de Querci haunts my imagination. But *your* felicity alleviates *my* uneasiness – as your joys or sorrows must

ever be reverberated on the heart of
    Your ladyship's obliged
      And affectionate nephew,
        MUNSTER.'

From Lady Eliza Finlay, to the Countess of Darnley.
                         London.

'My Dear Aunt,

This is a place I often wished to come to, but the peaceful satisfaction I have had in your company makes me in vain find it in your absence – everything I see, everything I hear, is so contrary to reason, that, without diverting one's self of that quality, it is impossible to be pleased with any thing, though the novelty may engage one's attention at first. All here appear to adopt the reigning ideas, and fashionable pursuits, with as much pleasure as I feel in conforming to the principles which your kind instructions and edifying example have implanted in my mind. They do not, however, appear to me to be happy, and, like comedians (who are not diverted with the amusement they occasion) regret being condemned to communicate a pleasure which they do not partake, and lament not having received, from a different education, other tastes, other talents, and other manners. I connect myself as little as possible with them; as in epidemic distempers we are only secure whilst we escape the touch of the contagious person; and with respect to wounds of the mind, they are like those of the body. These extravagancies I might, perhaps, some months ago have considered in a less serious manner, but the evident melancholy in which my brother is, shews me the vanity of everything in this world — So handsome in his person, so accomplished in his manners – possessing every- thing the world places a value on – and yet too apparently wretched. The Marquis of P———, Lord Sombre, and his other friends, endeavour in vain to rouse him out of his *reveries*. – You are possessed of such philosophy, that you may look upon this matter in another light; as for me, who have *strong passions*, and that inseparable companion of them, *weak reason*, I cannot help being seriously alarmed. My beloved brother has undoubtedly some secret cause of disquietude – he sighs at times as if his heart would break! This affects me very sensibly; I never was so unhappy in my life; besides, I have not my dear Aunt to give a friendly check to my extravagance of spirits, so am afraid of hazarding anything. — Every person looks formally at me. When your friend the Duchess of W——— introduced me to Lady Charlotte Sombre, she said she pleased herself with thinking what a harmony would arise between us; for in the character, said she, I drew *of her* to you, she only sat *for yours*. Lady Charlotte is very agreeable, lively, and entertaining. Lord Sombre, I fancy, is what you would esteem a superior character; he is noble, and has a soul; a thing questioned much in most of the gay youths whom we converse with. He appears to have fine feelings – I intend to be on my guard before him — a man of true taste and delicacy prefers the smile of the soul, to noisy mirth.

Lady Charlotte is addressed by Sir Alexander French – he told her, his love would be eternal! That is, said she, neither to have *beginning* nor *end*. Sir Alexander is a very great coxcomb, she therefore gives him no encouragement; and amused me with an account of him – her brother checked her, and said there is an ostentation in these kind of confidences, which he was mortified to observe in her – that at least she should respect a man she had rendered unhappy, and who had almost lost his reason on her account. She replied, it were indeed a trifling sacrifice, were it even so, as he had so little to part with, that it made the loss inconsiderable – love, said she, never makes such a bustle in hearts like his – his is a *laughing*, not a *melancholy* Cupid. She has the charms of an angel, and dresses with the greatest simplicity, regarding the colour and make of her cloaths, rather than the quality.

When Lady Charlotte shewed me the *Arcadia* of my mother's painting*, all the tender passions were up in my soul: I requested to be left alone, and bursting into tears, I partly relieved the emotions of my heart — Lord Sombre surprised me in this situation – I was too much agitated at

* See Vol. I. Page 47.

first to return him an answer to some obliging things he said, but at last made an apology for my weakness! His Lordship told me, the sensibility I testified confirmed him in the high ideas he entertained of my character. He then expatiated to me on a subject very agreeable, *my mother's virtues*. That the gentleman who educated him had been well acquainted with her – who said, that good sense and genius were united in her, and that by study, reflection, and application, she had improved her talents in the happiest manner — having acquired a superiority in thinking, speaking, writing, and acting — and in manners, her behaviour, language, and understanding, were inexpressibly charming.

The discourse of people here, my dear Aunt, appears to me malicious; their civilities feigned; their confidences false; and their friendships resemble a rose, which pricks the hand of him who smells it. Every animal seeks its food, digs itself a hole, or builds itself a nest – sleeps – and dies. It is a melancholy reflection that the greatest part of mankind do *no more*. The employment which distinguishes them most from other animals, is the care of cloathing themselves, and their enmity to each other – the first of these engages the attention of millions of the younger people in this great city – while the more aged employ themselves in the last. Although pride is observable in a peacock and a horse, passion, in a tiger, gluttony in a wolf, envy in a dog, laziness in a monkey, and treachery in a cat, yet one does not find, in any animal whatever, falseness to their own species.

A love of play, and building, are the characteristics of this age — our sex imitates the other as far as they can in the former – and having no *terra firma* for the latter, and not contented with the ancient custom of castle-building, erect fabrics on their heads three stores high. The rage of building is so great, that nothing can check their ardour in it, although it has been the ruin of many individuals; and there are at present (it is said) fifteen hundred uninhabited houses in the two parishes of Saint Mary-le-bone and Pancras. Though the fortunes of most individuals are decreased in value by the rise of the prices of provisions, and other articles of expense, yet the houses, good enough twenty years ago, are now judged inadequate. Among many other reasons alledged for this, every woman of any tolerable fashion requires a room for her wardrobe: what formerly could be kept in a chest, occupies the space of a large apartment, as gowns (on account of their trimmings) cannot be folded.

In short, my dear Aunt, all seem to walk in a vain show, and the curls of *the head* are more attended to, than the sensations of *the heart*.

I hope Mrs Dorothea Bingley is become more reasonable than to wish to force my dear friend's inclination to marry a man she detests. Don't you think, my dear aunt, that marrying to increase love, is like gaming to become rich; they only lose what little stock they had before.

My brother desires his respectful compliments to you, as I beg mine may be acceptable to your Lord; and I ever am, with the greatest esteem,

>   Your ladyship's affectionate,
>   And obliged niece,
>   ELIZA FINLAY.

From the Countess of Darnley to
Lady Eliza Finlay

My Dear Niece,

As in my present situation* I am interdicted from writing – I shall only indulge myself in a few words to you. The civilities you have received from all friends give me great pleasure. Brought up in the lap of friendship, I am not surprised, that upon your first emerging into the great world you should feel the coldness of the common address of strangers. It is possible those very accomplishments which delighted your fond aunt and friends, *interested* for your welfare, procure you the envy of *uninterested observers*. But if any one denies you the praises your merit claims, betray not any mortification at their want of candour, as your sensibility would afford them a malicious pleasure.

I have ever made it a rule, before I vexed myself about people's appearing to slight me, to consider the character of the person, and to discover the motives of his acting; and I

---

* She expected to lay in every day.

very often found it was with no design to affront me, but that the party was so humoursome as even to be insupportable *to himself.* I have so long indulged myself in the society of a few friends I love, that I am but ill suited for the world, as anything unreasonable *vexes me*, and the want of sincerity *offends me*. Mrs Dorothea Bingley continues to persecute her niece on account of Mr Bennet! Nothing appears to me so barbarous. I feel myself the happiest of women, and of wives, and enjoy my felicity with a double *goût*, by reflecting upon the restrictions I put on my inclinations for so many years. And I am perfectly convinced, it is not until women have got over their early years, that they can taste the delightful pleasure of loving and being beloved. But no felicity is perfect in this world, and I find my joy allayed from the observations I made on your brother's apparent melancholy. To see you and him happy, and properly allied, are circumstances I still must look forward to with great anxiety. I am very apt to believe man a much greater machine than he is generally supposed to be. "Whoever (says Dr Johnson) shall inquire by what motives he was determined on important occasions, will find them such as his pride will scarcely suffer him to confess; some sudden ardour of desire, some uncertain glimpse of advantage, some petty competition, some inaccurate conclusion, or some example implicitly reverenced."

Such are too often the causes of our resolves. Rousseau says, if you would understand the men, study the women – I myself think that it is difficult to know what a man's conduct will be, until you are acquainted with his wife's character, particularly when he enters into that connexion at an early period of his life.

My best affections ever attend you and your brother, in which my lord most sincerely joins.

FRANCES DARNLEY.

From Miss Bingley to Lady Eliza Finlay.

'Dear Madam,
Agreeable to your desire I write you a long letter in hopes of making you laugh (for your letter to me gave me the vapours, you appeared so serious, so unlike yourself) — it is

probable I may not effect my intention; but it will be a proof to you of my affection. My aunt has been even rude to Sir James Mordaunt, told him that he need not presume on my partiality for him, that I had nothing to say in regard to disposing of myself – that he must *treat with her*. He answered her with some heat, that he had no idea of modern marriages, where their lawyer is the priest that joins them; and the banns of matrimony are the indentures, land and ring — That in short he had no notion of treating for a wife as he would buy stock of a broker – that if she chose to give me her fortune, it *was well* – if not, we could live *without it!* lovers you know, my dear Lady Eliza, are always philosophers! — Your fortune, answered my good aunt, won't be a superfluous maintenance for a family, and you shall not have a shilling of mine! Very true, returned Sir James; but where content attends a competency more is *unnecessary*.

I hope, said she, you are in the court party and may get a pension? Sir James told her he was not; but if he were it would be worse for him, as the principles by which the court govern themselves are literally these: The man who has trumpeted their merits for years, cannot on any provocation assume an opposite character, without impeaching his judgment and proving the instability of his attachment — Our enemies it is wisdom to buy; but our friends will either be firm in our cause from motives of interest, or silent sufferers from motives of pride – Therefore, said he, good madam, laughing, I mean to rise by being *in the opposition* – as most of the great men have done before me! but, turning to me, said, I never yet opened my mouth in that celebrated assembly, but to give utterance to an occasional little monosyllable: But I may improve in time.

My aunt detains Mr Bennet for hours together, as Aristæus held Proteus to deliver oracles, judging I shall be charmed with his learning and oratory; but I should like him infinitely better if she would imitate Dulness, who kept the Muses in the Dunciad to silence them. But for this eternal teazer's *presence*, and your *absence*, (which by the by increased my consequence) I should have enjoyed the races very much. Mrs Damer, on whom nature has bestowed an understanding greatly superior to her form, confesses you are handsome;

whilst Miss Maydew, who has no other ambition than that of attracting applause by the charms of her person, allows you good sense. We seldom withhold the applause which is due to virtues or accomplishments for which we cannot value ourselves.

As to news, Mrs Trevors is parted with her husband: she put the poor man out of all patience by her sameness of character: If he made an observation, she assented; if he altered his mind, she gave a nod. She was always the same tune, the same object, that is to say *the same woman*. Perfectly agreed, no quarels indeed subsisted between them, but they *fell asleep*. Water freezes only in stagnation. Indifference hung over them like a cloud, and irksome passed the hours, which might have flown with a swift pace, perhaps, had they been passed with your humble servant.

The world would have been already laid in ruins if the elements that compose it did not maintain it by their discordant concord. If water did not resist fire by its coldness and humidity it would have reduced all into ashes, and having no further nutriment would have consumed itself. I will not lose Sir James's heart from this cause. Diversity of opinions shall quicken our conversation — Opposition shall not be wanting on my part to cheer *his heart*, and make his time pass *aggreeably*. An accommodating temper is all a man ought to expect in a wife; more than this is disgusting – I am very apt to believe that though a man of spirit would not suffer his wife to dictate to him, yet he would as soon talk to a parrot, or be the companion of a monkey, as of one who is his eccho on every occasion. It is very possible with some men to be *too good*. But there are no rules without exceptions; for was my husband very perverse I would (follow the late example of the *Premier** with the Opposition) revenge myself on him by agreeing in opinion with him, which would oblige him to commence hostilities with himself if he meant to *continue the dispute*.

Our ancient neighbour Lady Ogle married the other day a young ensign in the guards, although you know she has more diseases than Galen ever wrote of – at every cough resigns

* In the conciliatory Measures proposed concerning America.

some of her teeth, and every night screws off her leg – scarcely has her own nose, and by the course of nature ought to have kneeled in marble, or lifted up her arms in stone twenty years ago. In apology for her conduct, she says, it was merely to procure herself *a friend*. But as experience does not coincide with her ladyship's expectations, I should marry Mr Bennet, to *get rid of him*, were it not for my penchant *elsewhere*. I look upon all these romantic notions of Platonic, or spiritual love, as highly ridiculous. Our passions were bestowed on us for wise purposes. When precepts of virtue are strained too high, they are either impracticable or become vicious in their consequences.

The captain, *her friend*, is contriving a *visto* through some *woods* on *her estate*, to pay *his debts*; she tells every body, however, that he is not only possessed of *all the graces*, but an independant fortune. The next heir to the estate happens to be of a different opinion – his picture of captain Plume is *all shade*, hers *all light*. The former awkwardly imitates the style of Rembrandt, and with a dark pencil loves to describe hideous wrinkles and deformed features – but the latter artfully copies the taste of Titian, and brightens the canvas with all the lively glow of colouring. Perhaps if light and shade were properly blended together, we might behold a real likeness. – I don't like him. I mistake much if he is not conceited – you know I pretend a little to be a physiognomist as well as a botanist. In the natural world the external form of plants afford us a hint for a conjecture of their virtues. Almost all the plants of the same kinds are of the same virtues. The poisonous plants, natives of our soil, are hardly a dozen, and these are characterized even to the eye by something singular or dismal in the aspect.

When I wrote you I was jealous of Sir James's attentions to Miss Ords, I did not wish to be understood *au piè du lettre* – She has a vacant countenance, her youth only renders her *passable*. Her wit is not picquante, nor her manners alluring. She can answer *yes* and *no*, with tolerable success, nay sometimes hazards further: and when she goes to a comedy does not intreat the company to instruct her *when* she should laugh. Her father lives *en Prince*: like Lucullus, he *plundered all Asia* to assist him *in house-keeping*. Sir James was very lively in his usual way – She said she did not like puns, and had never made one in her life – I could not help answering – It's my opinion *you never will*.

You ask me if I have got no more lovers? To talk ingenuously with you – no; I know not what further inconveniences such an acquisition might put me to: and as it might probably happen (not on *my account*, but for my *aunt's acres*) I have whispered my passion for Sir James Mordaunt as a secret to Mrs M———; so you need not doubt but it has spread. She is an antiquated virgin, who endeavours to make chastity atone for the want of every other virtue. She wanted me sadly to ask her some question; I mortified my own curiosity, to punish her propensity to detraction.

Lady Dun is at last expired, notwithstanding the prayers of the faithful. Had she lived any longer, her *piety* must have ruined *her family* by her total want of economy, as she did the reputation of her neighbours by scandal.

> *Can so much gall in holy breasts reside?*
> Boileau's Lutrin. Canto I.

I met the following story lately in an old book; the writer appears to have been a person of great judgment, and not in *the least* given to credulity. He relates, that a certain man who had a wife that made this world his purgatory (though, according to the *common acceptation*, she was *virtuous* and prudent) happening to die some little time after her, he went to paradise, as soon as the breath was out of his body, as a reward for his patience in this world; being come to the gate, he knocks, the good man St Peter opens the door, and desires him very civilly to walk in, and take what seat in heaven he pleased. The husband stopped a moment to recollect himself; and then asks St Peter, Whether or not his wife was there? The good Saint answered in the affirmative: upon which the honest man, without staying for any thing further, takes to his heels and makes for the road to hell; rather choosing to renounce heaven, than be in the same place with his dear rib, whom he was well assured would, out of the abundance of her virtue, make heaven as great a hell to him, as she had done this earth.

I must now, my dear friend, tell you what sincerely grieves

me. My brother equals *yours* in melancholy: before he went abroad, no man whatever had better spirits; but now, although he does not complain of any particular disorder, yet is he always indisposed – ever wretched, constantly sighing and lamenting. This affects my spirits much: "*my heart is not of that rock, nor my soul careless as that sea, which lifts its blue waves to every blast, and rolls beneath the storm!*" But truth obliges me to confess that I cannot go on with my admired poet as – "*The virgins* have not as yet *beheld me silent in the hall!*" No, no no, it is not come to that yet! I relieve you from my company – be sensible of the obligation – let me hear from you soon, and believe me,

> Your ladyship's
> > affectionate friend,
> > > H. BINGLEY.'

From Lady Eliza Finlay to Miss Bingley.

'My dear Harriot,

Many thanks for your agreeable letter, your *gaieté de coeur* always pleases me, *Vive la bagatelle!*

But, my dear friend, I am uneasy at your aunt's persisting in her persecution of you on Mr Bennet's account. He seems to me to be a person rather created to fill up a vacuum in nature, than to perform any active good in it. His want of sensibility is sufficient to prepossess me against him – There are in the occurrences of a married life so many trials of a man's humanity that he whose want of tenderness might pass unobserved had he continued single – must often appear a very monster considered as a husband. May you be blessed in that state with the man of your heart! I agree with you that opposition, carried on without violence, gives a dignity to our condescension; but we must not carry this too far or we may counteract our design of preserving the heart we have gained.

To manage men requires more dexterity than to win them, as the consequence of most *love matches* evinces.

You ask a thousand questions, having never been in London yourself, on account of your aunt's apprehensions of a disease she had not the resolution of giving you at an early period of life*. I told you that you must not expect any characters from me, as I was always an enemy to detraction, and few there are that merit commendation. Let us, my dear friend, regulate our *own conduct*, rather than condemn that *of others*: but as I cannot refuse you anything you ask (though I may wonder at your asking) I will suppose we are chatting over a dish of tea, and giving our opinion of a gown or a cap, and will tell you who suits my taste, or who my reason contemns, with as little meaning as if I talked of the gown and not the woman: and this I the more readily do, as I know you will not betray the confidence I place in you.

The truth is, however, I am perfectly astonished at the strange characters this town abounds with; and stupified (*if I may* be allowed the expression) with what I have heard: but, as Shakespeare allows Desdemona to speak after she was smothered, you will permit me to write though I have lost my understanding. And as it was the choice of certain great men to be intelligible, it is probable my present state of mind will lead me to imitate them. But on second thoughts, my being not *au fait* to the subject may perhaps make me excel in it. Men often expatiate *best* on what they *least understand*, by the same rule that people in general are contrary to what they would seem.

The Mantuan Swain lived constantly at court: Horace wrote in celebration of a country life when he resided in Rome: and it is well known travels, voyages, etc. to every part of the world have been written in London. Why should I not then, Eliza Finlay Spinster, attempt delineating manners, which I have really seen? My scruples would intrude – that perhaps I am not sufficiently informed, as I have only resided here a month; but these vanish on the recollection that I must certainly be in the right in the above position – Otherwise, could it be possible for Mr Blacklock†, a poet blind from his birth, to describe visible objects with more spirit and justness, than others blessed with the most perfect sight? Could certain

---

* The difference in the degrees of danger between suffering a person to take the small pox in the natural way, and communicating it by innoculation, is upon the lowest computation estimated *thirty* to *one* in favor of innoculation.

† Mr Blacklock may, in reality, be regarded as a prodigy – He is a man of a most amiable character, of singular ingenuity, and of very extraordinary attainments.

orators, famous for their *extravagance*, harangue on *economy* –
Or the learned at Venice employ father Piaggi to copy the
manuscript found at Herculaneum (though he is unacquain-
ted with Greek, the language they are written in) – Or could
our own countrymen, the *learned, judicious* body in Warwick-
lane, refuse to admit to be their associates in the science of
Æsculapius, any but those who have studied where – *medicine
is not taught?* After such precedents as these, it is clear I
cannot err, in informing you of what – *I know little about*.
Besides, it is an established rule of prudence, on the contrary,
never to commit yourself by talking or writing on a subject the
world gives you the credit of understanding, as you have
nothing to *gain* but *much* to *lose*. This consideration no doubt
induced one author* to omit in his tragedy *morality*, which
should be the ground-work of every fable, and deterred
another* from acknowledging providence, though it so
eminently presided, and was so conspicuously displayed in
the miraculous escapes made in the voyages he wrote of. This
being premised, I will now begin boldly to *relate* many things I
cannot *comprehend*.

Miss Ton accompanied me to the opera; I was amazed at
the height of her head, and how her chair had failed to crush
the fabric of feathers and frivolity which rose above each
other! I could not think she had flown, though she was
composed of cork and feather; and willing to be informed
how she had managed it (as ignorance, you know, is
reprehensible) I ventured to ask her the question. She
returned me a look of contempt (as if to pity my ignorance)
saying, she always took care to prevent a misfortune of that
kind! When I go to court, said she, as heads are wore lower†
there — I fit like your old woman upon the seat of the chair,
which is convenient enough on account of one's trimmings,
but when I go to the opera, where *fancy directs* and *fashion
prevails*, I say my prayers the whole way – that is to say, I
kneel *on the bottom of the chair*. I admired her ingenuity; only
observed, I hoped it did not fatigue her knees so much as to

---

* Both clergymen.
† In compliment to the Queen, who has too much good sense to approve of what is
ridiculous.

prevent her from going to church next day! O, not in the least, said she; but I always go to the drawing-room of a Sunday! except when I go to the Chapel-royal – *the closet there*, indeed, that is no bad public place – nobody but people of fashion are admitted, and it is really sometimes very amusing! The truth is, if one liked church very much, there is time enough to dress afterwards; for it is not *the rage* which a certain set to go to the drawing-room until your old-fashioned people are coming away. Oh the dear delight of meeting these dowdies on their *retour* home to their spouses and family dinners at *four o'clock*. Then we make such glorious confusion! I took the liberty of saying that I thought the respect due to their Majesties had induced every body to be in the drawing-room previous to their appearance! Oh, not at all, child, said she – except your *formal ones!* But why, said I, madam, need you go to court of a Sunday, why not of a Thursday as well? Of a Thursday! Nobody goes of a Thursday! Pardon me, replied I, the Duchess of W——— introduced me on that day! That may be, replied Miss *Ton*, her Grace is very old, wrinkles make her religious – but none but such, or courtiers, go of a Thursday! I again took the liberty of telling her that it had also been a very full drawing-room — Then, said she, it must have been the Thursday after the birthday – or some particular day; for otherwise few of a certain set, who understand *the rage*, would go. The *rage*, said I, madam! I am again at a loss; did I hear you right? O, perfectly well, said she; the *ton*, was formerly the word, but *the rage*, has lately been adopted from the French! (It is to be hoped, that the Parisians will also, from their late partiality for *English Gauzes, Silks, Linens, etc.* induce us to adopt *them also*, instead of too often procuring these articles from France.)

Forgetful of the imprudence I was going to commit — I told Miss *Ton* her prayers had proved ineffectual – her largest feather was snapped in two. Is it possible! exclaimed she, and reddened prodigiously. – Shocked at the blunder I had made, and pitying her weakness, I gave her my bottle of Eau de Luce; and not caring to hazard any further on so interesting a subject, lest it should hurt her nerves, I turned the conversation to what was more indifferent – a sister of her's, who *had died in child-bed a fortnight before*.

(This, my dear friend – to philosophise – no abstract evil exists; for whatever calamities human life is subject to, their evil depends merely on our own sensibility.)

Sir Timothy Clinquant rejoined us. He is handsome, has a good opinion of himself, and is no stranger to the art of flattery. She lamented to him the accident of her feather. From a knowledge of human nature, that nothing pleases so much as to have a defect of any kind turned into a beauty — he assured her the feather being broke gave it an air of negligence so perfectly adapted to the *contour* of her fine face, that he could not be convinced, but that she *accidentally* on *purpose* afforded it *that grace*. Thus was she restored to good-humour. – I can tell you little of what I saw; Miss Ton's head intercepted my view of the stage: *her rage* of going late having prevented our getting any other but end seats, and she sat before me. In the reign of Queen Elizabeth there was a law made to restrict the growth of ruffs: I wish our legislators,* who, in this accommodating age, do sometimes condescend to bestow their attention on trifles, would take the size of heads into their consideration. Mr Walpole observes, in his anecdotes of painting in England, that in the reign of the two first Edwards, the ladies erected such pyramids on their heads that the face became the center of the body.

An eminent physician has declared, that more deformed children have been brought into the world this last year than for twenty years before, on account of the ladies stooping in their carriages – One thing I am certain of – it makes them contract a habit of frowning, that furrows their foreheads.

A fine lady is the least part of herself, and is every morning put together like some instrument. Dress is the subject eternally discussed. Gulliver tells us, that the sages of Laputa, having substituted things in place of words, carried along with them such things as were necessary to express the particular business they intended to discourse on. – Were this the case, it would be a great relief; but alas! they do no more here than propose the subject. But to return to the opera – Miss *Ton*, in

---

* Witness the purchase of a collection of antique and Etruscan vases, by the public money – and their enacting a lottery for toys.

telling me who the people were, said they were *horrid creatures*, that is to say, censorious or *awkward*, because *not of her particular set*.

But what was my surprise to perceive her familiarly afterwards whispering to one, curtsying to another, telling a third how unfortunate she had been in not being at home when she did her the honor of calling on her! I could not help testifying my astonishment at her conduct! – She laughed, and said – I am civil to those people, as the Indians worship the devil – *for fear*. Besides, said she, the last Lady has a rich brother lately come from India. In days of yore women married for a title, a fine seat, etc. – A title is very agreeable, but a *fine seat*, the very idea of it gives me the vapours! I would rather marry a London justice than a lord lieutenant of the county. It did very well formerly (when people were so dull as to be able to bear their own thoughts) to live moping at an old family place; but manners are *now* too much improved for *that*: and a nabob's cash, without the append-ages of the seats of his ancestors, will suffice to carry me one season to Spa, another to Tunbridge, etc. etc. – In marrying a nabob, there is a moral security of never being buried in the country. I am no *devot*, but I believe there is such a thing as conscience; and, as few of these continental heroes can bear to listen to their silent monitor – it induces them to lead *exactly the kind of life I like* – to *exclude reflection!*

I answered, that she was too severe; I made no doubt but that a man may get rich across the Atlantic, without wounding his honor, and all the finer feelings of humanity by peculation and extortion, which leaves the possessors more wretched than pale-eyed poverty with all its whole train of meagre haunts. To change the conversation, I said, so madam, I find you intend to marry. Yes, said she, *to be sure* – But I hope in god I shall have no children to *spoil my shape*. I cannot here refrain from telling you a circumstance I saw occur myself. We dined at Lady ———'s; I observed a lady change colour – Mrs. ——— whispered to her, that ladies in her situation (for she appeared with child) were apt to be *indisposed*. She seemed hurt at the supposition, and denied any thing was the matter with her! As by the conversation it appeared she had *already had children*, I was at a loss to account for *her conduct*. Colonel H———, her husband, appeared very uneasy – an inquisitive look of kindness, a tender affectionate concern, were strongly depicted on his manly countenance — his anxiety appeared to me to proceed from that fond attachment arising from loving another better than one's self. I entered into his ideas, contemplated her happiness, and as he is not a very young (though agreeable) man, the apparent attention he paid her confirmed me in what you know was always my sentiments, that *such* make the *best husbands*. Desirous of relieving his anxiety by contributing to her ease, I begged she would permit me to accompany her to another apartment. As her uneasiness had greatly increased – she was under a necessity of accepting my offer – and fainted as soon as she got into Mr.———'s library. The alarmed and fond husband followed, who intreated a maid might be called to cut the lacing of her stays. He was much affected, and, addressing Lady Charlotte Sombre and me, said, There, young ladies, lies a victim of the fashion! Before I brought her to this town – she was the delighted mother of three fine children – but these fond sensations are now lost in the trifling consideration of a *fine shape*; and though in the last month of her pregnancy, she has a vanity in flattering herself she cannot be thought in *that situation!* The lady was carried home, and we heard next day she had been delivered of a *still-born child*.

Lord Spangle asked Miss *Ton*, how soon she got to bed the other morning? Not, my Lord, until eight – you know we did not sit down to dinner until twelve at night. Not until twelve at night! said I. No, returned she; you know nobody dines till after the opera: it was *Danzi's* benefit; all the world were there, and there were many songs *encored*. — Dinner was ordered by eleven; but Lady Peccedillo was not at the opera – her monkey died, and she had not nerves for seeing Lord ——— who is always there, and who she esteems the direct image of her dead favourite. Her hair-dresser was ordered at ten, but disappointed her – and dinner was retarded on her account. Pray, said I, at what time did you sup? Why, we sat down to cards at two o'clock, played until six, then went to supper, and parted half an hour after seven! I find, said I, that the people of the *ton* reckon the time according to the *Mosaic* custom, where the evening and the morning make the day. But pray, madam, what becomes of your servants all this time? I hope you only appoint them to attend you home? Servants! Lord, Madam, nobody thinks of their servants! I do not see myself what business servants have to sleep *at all!* I can do very well with three hours sleep, and I expect next winter to bring myself to two*!

You say that lady and Mrs. ———— have been lately abused, even by their own friends, that is to say – those they associated most with – Would you know the reason? My dear friend, they have left off play, at which they generally lost considerably. The first of these ladies, from unavoidable misfortunes, altered her plans in life: the last, from a different cause — Her family remonstrated, her husband frowned; but they remonstrated, and he frowned to *no purpose!* Her luck turned, her passion increased for that dangerous amusement, yet she took a resolution, and would *play no more.* – She who was before set down as an agreeable acquaintance, was now deemed capricious, and the eyes of her card-playing acquaintances, who were before *blind* to her *real imperfections*, became now *scrupulously attentive* to her *imaginary errors*. Many various conjectures were formed for the reasons of her conduct – many allegations made that she had formed *an attachment*, or was deterred by *spouses's directions!* To clear her at once from these imputations, neither of which (be they *crimes or virtues*) she has a mind capable of – The truth is – she has beautiful teeth – and accidentally read Mr Tolver's book, where he considers the passions as internal causes of their diseases.

Errors proceeding from the *sensations of the heart*, are not *those* of this age. I was told there had been a long attachment between Lady ———— and Colonel ————. I deplored, I pitied her! He is now abroad in a dangerous situation! What anxiety, what wretchedness must she not suffer! How

---

* Thus do many women sacrifice their healths, without considering it is in vain to conquer nature. Man can subsist but for a determinate space only asleep or awake – by continual watching the incessant motion of the fibres would destroy their organic elasticity, and prevent their future reparation; and by continual sleeping, though the fibres are not fatigued, the nervous fluid would be gradually exhausted by the action of the organs of life, and would never be repaired.

surprised I was to find – she never misses *a public place*. The Duchess of W——— was much amused at my simplicity – Formerly (said she) if a woman had the misfortune *to love where* she could not avow it – decency induced her carefully to conceal her weakness – but now it is *quite otherwise* – The soft sensations find no admittance into their sophisticated hearts – though they have no objection to a man of fashion *in their train*. – And a certain set of *the ton*, or *the rage* go so far as even studiously to afford an appearance *of what* in reality never entered into *their imaginations!*

I think I hear you say, how strange! But everything is so I think in this place. I met Lady Bab Cork-rump the other day: My dear Lady Eliza, said she, I love a comedy of all things; pray let us go to one soon. I am disengaged next Thursday — That is very lucky, returned I; I have *a box that evening: it is our favourite play*; and *Mrs Abington acts!* – That is *delightful*, said she! And, added I, it is a charity play for the dispensary of the infant poor — upwards of twenty-six thousand children have been relieved by this humane institution since its commencement nine years ago. Lady Bab heard the above impatiently. – It is a charity play, you say, madam! – I don't know, I believe my brother expects some friends from the country. I suppose it will be no disappointment to your ladyship if I *don't go?* – O, not in the least, said I — Thus the idea of *Charity* makes a fine lady shrink (as if it were contagious) into herself, and prevented Lady Bab from going to a place her inclination otherwise induced her to.

Lady Bab seems to have a great partiality for Sir Hugh, our neighbour — Since he got his fortune – his riots are generosity – carelessness, the freedom of his soul – his prodigalities, an easiness of mind proportioned to his estate. He quarrelled the other day with Captain Essence on her account; and I was alarmed to the greatest degree for the consequences! she laughed at my fears, assuring me there was no kind of danger in what I apprehended. The gentlemen, said she, have renounced the conduct of heroes. The custom of wagers is the happy succedaneum, and prevents much blood-shed. Thus matters of dispute are left in *tranquil doubt*, until the period arrives for *its* no less *tranquil decision*. It turned out as she said; Captain Essence wagered with Sir Hugh, that *the new club in Saint James's Street would be the ruin of Lord —* , *before the old one vis-à-vis had knocked up General —* .

I have spent so much money on *bagatelles*, that I cannot help regretting the expenditure of what if otherwise applied might have produced such beneficial effects. – But if we commit some follies, we are sufficiently kept in countenance by the other sex. Modern story tells us the late King of Poland was so much captivated with forty-eight china vases, that he purchased them of the late King of Prussia at the price of a *whole regiment of dragoons*.

You know, my dear friend, how many elogiums have been bestowed on Lady Darnley, on account of the aids she afforded for the disquisition of the particular genius's which distinguished the young people, to prevent a misapplication of the talents of the rising generation. "Is it not by a misapplication of talents," said one, "that our present mortifications arise? Many a man miscarrying in one profession, would have succeeded happily in another. Hence we see so many heads applied to what requires thinking, which might have been applied to their country's good in the manner of the ancient use of *battering rams*, and have been run against stone walls *without the least danger of being hurt*. – If the mechanic should invert all the principles which compose the knowledge of that science; if he should assign the wheels to be the principle of motion, the spring to run round and be moved, the weight to vibrate and regulate, and the pendulum to urge; would not all mankind deride such a machine, because it could not perform its office? Is not this the unhappy case of this country at present? have not our enemies taken the advantage of it?"

But to leave politics – which I owe to the observations of an old gentleman, who has too much reason to be chagrined with the procrastination in the conduct of public affairs, as it has affected the interest of his private family – I am most sincerely concerned on account of your aunt's apparent obstinacy in favour of Mr Bennet. Parents, imagining that years *impart wisdom*, which have only *altered tastes*, are apt to be arbitrary in their determinations, and dress in the furs, which become the ice of old-age, the glowing blood of youth.

But do not, my dear friend, barter your happiness for splendour. I suppose (but do not take my supposition for an oracle) that it is not likely I shall every marry – If I do not, my fortune shall be yours; being ever most affectionately

Your sincere friend
ELIZA FINLAY.

From the Earl of Munster to the
Countess of Darnley.

My dear Aunt,

Since I wrote you last, I walked one day in the city. A *black man, well dressed*, fell down in the street: as none was near, I run, took him in my arms, and carried him into a house of refreshment, where I immediately procured him assistance. Upon his recovery he acknowledged his obligations to me, and said, that but for me he must have died:— and at the end of the lottery of life, our last minutes, like benefit tickets left in the wheel, rise in their valuation. I accompanied him home, where I saw his wife; who, though as black as the collyed night, is as ingenious, sensible, and agreeable a woman as can be found among the daughters of England. He inquired of her for a friend; who arriving, to my inexpressible surprise proved to be the Marquis de Villeroy, but so emaciated that the eye of friendship could not behold him without shedding tears – he knew me at once, and ran to my embrace — This, said he to the black gentleman, is Lord Munster, my friend, the companion of my youth.

After the joy we mutually testified at meeting, I could not help testifying my surprise at the alteration in his person! My Lord, replied he, I will acquaint you with the most extraordinary history that ever occurred to any one. Upon the receipt of your letter, I made no doubt, in the first impulse of passion, but you had betrayed me; I suddenly left the army, and travelled day and night until I took shipping for Rotterdam. On my arrival at that place, I found my father had left it; and was also informed of the honorable part you had acted, and that I had falsely flattered myself with the Countess's affection. I lamented your misfortune and my impatience, as on reflection I was sensible of the imprudence I had committed in leaving my post — I was determined, however, not to lie under any imputation of cowardice – I returned to — waited on the general officer – acquainted him with the real truth, obtained forgiveness of my fault, which was afterwards looked upon in a proper light, as I had the good fortune to distinguish myself soon after in two engagements. Upon our being ordered into winter-quarters, I obtained leave of absence, and was resolved if possible to discover to what place my father had retired; for although my love was hopeless, I flattered myself still with having it in my power to rescue the Countess de Sons from his *tyranny*, and restore her *to you*.

My servant one day, with a face of joy, communicated to me that he had learned my father lived at a house near Marseilles. He heard this, he said, from a brother, who had an intrigue with one of the Duchess's maids. – Is the duke then married? said I. – Alas, my friend, said the Marquis, I am sorry to inform you, the object of your affections fell a victim to my father's designs – he compelled her to give him her hand! – I found he had turned the Countess's fortune into cash and jewels, on which he lived, being desirous of concealing the place of his abode, jealous to the last degree of her being seen! With this view all his servants *were females*.

Notwithstanding these precautions, his domestics talked of his peculiarities; which occasioned interrogatories concerning his funds of expense. These the inquirers soon discovered were in specie in the house: this determined them to rob him. My servant's brother, who was courting the Duchess's maid, informed her *of me*; next day received a letter from my sister, who promised to admit me one night into the house, where she directed me to come in disguise with my servant! – Thus was I made a tool of by these ruffians: they meant to effect the robbery by *my means*; and if detected, flattered themselves they would be pardoned *on my account!* At the time appointed I went; Julia let me in, leaving the door open for my servant. She was beginning to inform me of all their distresses, when our ears were assaulted by an alarm-bell! – in an instant the house was filled with people; I heard my father say, Where is the rascal who calls himself my son? My servant, upon being discovered, had informed him, that I had hired him and his three companions (whom he had introduced into the house) to murder and rob him, and to carry off the ladies! It was in vain I assured him to the contrary; he would not hearken to me; he recollected how much I had been in love with his charming ward; he upbraided me with my wickedness, and perhaps did believe me guilty.

This affair, I make no doubt, has been misrepresented in the world — we have no true histories, but such as have been written by those who were sincere enough to relate what they experienced, in what relates to themselves.

I was seized, and carried to a dungeon until my trial; when, without a hearing, I was condemned for life to be a galley-slave, and sent for that purpose on board the gallies at Marseilles. The labour of a *galley-slave*, is become a proverb; nor is it without reason that this may be reckoned the greatest fatigue that can be inflicted on wretchedness.

Imagine six men chained to their seats, entirely naked as when born, sitting with one foot on a block of timber fixed to the footstool; the other lifted up against the bench before them, holding in their hands an oar of an enormous size. Imagine them lengthening their bodies, their arms stretched out to push the oar over the backs of those before them; who are also themselves in a similar attitude. Having thus advanced their oar, they raise that end which they hold in their hands, to plunge the opposite in the sea; which done, they throw themselves back upon their benches below, which are somewhat hollowed to receive them. But none but those who have seen them labour can conceive how much they endure: none but such could be persuaded that human strength could sustain the fatigue which they undergo for an hour successively. But what cannot necessity and cruelty make men do? Almost impossibilities. Certainly no galley can be navigated in any other way, than by a crew of slaves, over whom a *comite* may exercise the most unbounded authority. No free man could continue at the oar an hour unwearied: yet a slave must sometimes lengthen out his toil for ten, twelve, nay, for twenty hours, without the smallest inter-mission. On these occasions the *comites*, or some of the other mariners, put into the mouths of those wretches a bit of bread steeped in wine, to prevent their fainting through excess of fatigue or hunger, while their hands are employed upon the oar. At such times are heard nothing but horrid blasphemies, loud bursts of despair, or ejaculations to Heaven; all the slaves streaming with blood, while their unpitying task-masters mix oaths and threats, and the smacking of whips, to fill up this dreadful harmony.

At this time the captain roars to the *comite* to redouble his blows; and when any one drops from his oar in a swoon, (which not unfrequently happens) he is whipped while any remains of life appear, and then thrown into the sea, without any farther ceremony. The *Diable Boitteux*, in order to make *Cleofas* sensible of the happy condition of an inquisitor, tells him, Was not I a Dæmon, I would be an inquisitor? Were the devil to become a mortal, he would incline to be the *comite* to the galley-slaves at Marseilles, whose hearts are inlapidated by cruelty.

How these slaves are fed, to enable them to support such enormous toil, may be judged from the following account. – When it was necessary we should take some refreshment, the captain ordered *the dogs to their mess*. He only meant by this, that we should be served with beans, the usual food allowed us. These are indeed most intolerable eating, and what nothing but the most pinching hunger could dispense with. They are ill boiled, with scarce any oil, a little salt, and all to be eaten out of a capacious cauldron, not the cleanest in the world, as may easily be conceived.

I was never so hungry but that I preferred eating my portion of bread dipped in vinegar and water to this mess, which even offended the sense of smelling. However, these, and twenty-two ounces of biscuit, are all the food allowed for a galley-slave. Each of the crew receives four ounces of this beverage; that is, provided none of it be secreted before it is brought upon deck, which is not unfrequently the case.

I once had the curiosity to count the number of beans which a brother slave had got for all his portion, which amounted to just thirty; and those of the little black bean, commonly called horse-beans. We did not even commiserate one another. To pity, we must be acquainted with the sufferings of our fellow-creatures, but not feel them. When we know by experience what pain is, we pity those who suffer; but when we ourselves are in pain, we then feel only what we ourselves undergo. In ever station, subject to the calamities of life, we allow to others that share of our sensibility only which we have no occasion for ourselves. People in ease, people in affluence, may think otherwise, but it is not *in nature*.

Dreadful as this was, I have always thought death a punishment that was no way adequate to the crimes of some public villians who have been punished with it; and I am certain the most cowardly among men, would prefer it to being a galley-slave. We are condemned to death by nature; the sentence of the law, and the hand of the hangman, only anticipate a few months or days; but to be daily wishing for death, as a friend, to relieve us, and to be debarred of all means of meeting him, is such a quintessence of wretchedness as would, I believe, make all mankind keep a strict guard upon their actions, that they may avoid falling into it.*

From this infernal state of existence I was delivered by Mr Worthy, who is a slave-merchant – he saw, and pitied my distress – he had accidentally saved the life of one of the ruffians who had assisted in the attempt to rob my father. This man afterwards, upon his death-bed, acquainted his good master of my situation, who promised to release me. This was effected by his giving a large sum to the captain and the *comite*. The secret was told me; it was agreed I should pretend to faint, and appear insensible; when I should be thrown into the sea as dead — This happily succeeded.

Nothing can be more unjust than to confine the instance of humanity within the narrow circle of a few European nations. The noble, the generous, the humane dispositions are diffused throughout all nature, and exert their engaging force wherever a body of men subsists. Virtue and vice are mingled in all societies: we have savages in Italy; and there are worthy men amongst those we call savages. Christians do often those things which a modest heathen would blush at, and, while they boast of their religion, are strangers to the common laws of humanity. It should be the boast of a wise man to despise nothing that he is not well acquainted with, and to do justice to all mankind, of whatever country or complexion. – Virtue,

---

* All misdemeanors are punished, among the Danes, by servitude in chains a longer or shorter time.

like the rays of the sun, shines over the whole habitable globe, enlivens the moral, as that the material world, and exerts its benign influences from the *scorching equinox* to the *frozen poles*. We feel its force; all communities saw, and pitied my distress – he had accidentally saved the life of one of the ruffians who had assisted in the attempt to rob my father. This man afterwards, upon his death-bed, acquainted his good master of my situation, who promised to release me. This was effected by his giving a large sum to the captain and the *comite*. The secret was told me; it was agreed I should pretend to faint, and appear insensible; when I should be thrown into the sea as dead — This happily succeeded.

Nothing can be more unjust than to confine the instances of humanity within the narrow circle of a few European nations. The noble, the generous, the humane dispositions are diffused throughout all nature, and exert their engaging force wherever a body of men subsists. Virtue and vice are mingled in all societies: we have savages in Italy; and there are worthy men amongst those we call savages. Christians do often those things which a modest heathen would blush at, and, while they boast of their religion, are strangers to the common laws of humanity. It should be the boast of a wife man to despise nothing that he is not well acquainted with, and to do justice to all mankind, of whatever country or complexion. – Virtue, like the rays of the sun, shines over the whole habitable globe, enlivens the moral, as that the material world, and exerts its benign influences from the *scorching equinox* to the *frozen poles*. We feel its force; all communities are bound together by its magnetic influence; and without it the nations of Barbary would be covered with devastation, and no more inhabited than the scorching sands of its inhospitable deserts.

Mr Worthy no sooner cast his eyes on me, and perceived my sorrow, than pity, tenderness, and compassion glowed in his countenance; his eyes moistened with generous sympathy, and the first word he spoke convinced me that he already felt *all I had suffered*. But there is no pleasure so transporting to him, as to be in any way instrumental in making any of the human species happy.

I acquiesced in the justice of these sentiments – and could

not sufficiently admire the fortitude which had supported the Marquis under such unheard-of trials! And as our sense of many high enjoyments, both natural and moral, is exceedingly heightened by our having observed or experienced many of the contary evils; he bids fair at least to be contented, when he looks back to the horrors he has escaped. The poet says,

> The heart can ne'er a transport know
> That never felt a pain.

It may easily be conceived the Marquis is most anxious to inquire after his family – but gratitude to Mr Worthy has made him accompany him to England.

When I seemed to compassionate his sufferings, his gratitude assumed a grateful humility; but the moment I appeared the least inattentive to his misfortunes, his countenance collected such an air of dignity, as not only reproached my seeming want of sensibility, but reminded me also, that his sufferings were not the consequences of guilt, nor could in the least degree lessen his greatness of mind.

I find Mr Worthy has a law-suit depending; when that is settled he is to accompany my friend to Italy. He appears to me a very acute, sensible man; – we were talking the other day of the disturbances at Madras, and of the strange conduct of the people in Leadenhall-Street – He said it put him in mind of Anacharsus's observation to Solon, as they were returning from a public assembly, 'That he could not help being greatly astonished to find, that, in their deliberations, it was the *wise that spoke*, and that *fools that decided*.' I believe, in public assemblies, this will be found generally to be the case, where party governs, and the most powerful cabal is generally composed of the least rational.

I attend these dear friends everywhere. The Marquis is an *amateur*, and his taste will be highly gratified, when at Munster-house, to view the prodigies of *your creation* – he is a descendant of the Medici family: consequently highly charmed with the character of the Countess of Darnley. But this is a subject, I am incapable of entering upon – to praise exquisite merit is perhaps the most difficult part of polite writing, and which I have no talents for; but which if I possessed, I should tire you with what few other ladies ever yet was – *their own praises*. But I will yield to none in what I value myself upon, being truly and affectionately.

    Yours
       MUNSTER

The Marquis de Villeroy became much enamoured with Lady Eliza, whose compassion for his misfortunes had so far softened her heart in his favor, that she listened to him first with complacency, afterwards with tenderness, and at last with the most lively interest. Congenial souls soon form an union. She acknowledged her partiality for him, but that no predilection whatever could induce her to leave her country and friends. This opinion was greatly strengthened by the idea she entertained of the inconstancy of mankind, and the little regard they pay to women after a few years possession.

The Marquis thought his renouncing his native country would be too great a sacrifice to be offered at the altar of the Graces. Yet the idea of parting with Lady Eliza was what he was unable to support. – She told him it would be in vain to think of making her soften the rigour of her decree; for it proceeded from a firmness, which nothing could conquer! for, from all her observations in life, no love ever lasted long enough to make it worth while to sacrifice every thing else to it; the *Paradisiac* vision of eternal constancy having long vanished from these sublunary regions:— and that unless he would reside in England – she never would be his! – A sigh, which stole from him, conveyed to Lady Eliza the height of his despair – his embarrassment and dejection increased her regard for him, while it awakened a tender commiseration for them, believing herself entirely the cause of them. She therefore thought it incumbent on her to endeavour to remove them by every attention in her power.– In consequence of this consideration in his favor, she strove to look cheerful, though she was not a little hurt at finding it absolutely necessary to reject so amiable and deserving a man.

The Marquis, perceiving that remonstrances would be ineffectual, took his leave with a heart distracted by grief, perplexity, and despair! Being naturally of a restless, gloomy disposition, and of violent passions, in his despair he thought his adventures had been so extraordinary that he was doomed to be wretched! and formed a resolution of laying violent hands on himself: and the more he meditated on his situation, the more strongly was he confirmed in his precipitate resolution. Yet, as the instinct of self-preservation is one of the strongest in our frame, it inspired him with a counter-idea, that of renouncing Italy; this only acquiescence being requisite to recommend him to Lady Eliza, without whom his life would be a burthen. He communicated his intentions to Lord Munster, who apprised his sister of this proof of the Marquis's attachment for her.

Flattered to the greatest degree at the strength of his affection, she promised to give him her hand on his return from Italy – where he must necessarily go, to prove the identity of his person, and to take possession of his fortune.

The Marquis made immediate preparations for his journey, and soon set out, accompanied by his friend Mr Worthy, Mrs Worthy accompanying Lady Eliza to Munster-house — Soon after their arrival Lord and Lady Darnley rejoined them with their little son, her ladyship being too tender a mother to leave him behind her, or to commit him to the care of any but herself. The tender brain of *Newton*, or *Alexander*, altered in their infancy by a small compression, or slight commotion, might have rendered the first stupid, and the other a wise King — Yet people in general, though emulous of obtaining wealth for their heirs, commit them to the care of uninterested hirelings. Sir Harry Bingley, his aunt and sister, and most of the parties already introduced to the reader, assembled at Munster house to spend the summer.

Mrs Lee had rejected every overture from her husband for a reconciliation, whilst his health and fortune lasted — but to a mind like hers, misfortunes cancelled every injury — His fortune ruined, his health impaired, he plunged deeper and deeper into every species of excess. This soon brought him to the greatest distress, and he was so much reduced as to be in want of the common necessaries of life. Mrs Lee, upon being informed of his deplorable situation, immediately converted that villa in Wales, of which there has been a description given*, into money, paid her husband's debts, and accompanied him at a wretched hovel, to which his poverty, the consequence of his crimes, and infidelity (*to her*) had reduced him. – There she continued, shewing him every attention until his decease; when she came with Lady Darnley to Munster-house.

* Vol. I. Page 165.

Lady Eliza soon received the following Letter from the Marquis de Villeroy.

Madam, Venice.

On my arrival at this place, I found that, on the report of my death, my father had consigned over his estate to a near relation of mine – who knew me at once, though so emaciated, and has acted in the most honorable manner to me. My father has retired to La-Trappe in France: thither my duty must lead me, previous to the happiness I shall receive in throwing myself at your feet.

Were I disposed to draw the most engaging *portrait* imaginable, I could easily find a subject; but as you may possibly wish for an intimate acquaintance with the original, I shall omit the attempt, since it would be difficult for you to obtain it from that principle in human nature which makes us strangers *to ourselves*.

I shall detain your ladyship no longer, than to request you will inform my friend, your brother, that I am mortified to be unable to deliver his letter to Mademoiselle de Querci — no such person can be found.

Need I paint that passion I have given you such proofs of? – No; all descriptions would fall short of my feelings. I will ever yield to every wish your soul can form; you are entirely absolute, unless you should attempt impossibilities, amongst which I reckon this as the greatest – for me to breathe a moment without being entirely and inviolably yours.

De Villeroy.

It may here be, perhaps, proper to inform the reader of what perhaps his own sagacity may have made him anticipate — The Duke de Salis had neither been able, by intreaties or threats, to compel the Countess de Sons to marry him, though he had given out that she had; this induced him to keep both her and his daughter closely confined. It has been already related, how he had consigned over his son as a house-breaker; – when he found him condemned to the gallies – like the cruel inconsistency of an

Admiral's* judges – he laid himself under the necessity of declaiming the equity of his own sentence – and when he found the decree against his son was inevitable – unable to bear the reproaches of his inward monitor, and listening to the whispers of a gloomy disposition, he became almost frantic — In this situation of mind, torn with the agonies of grief, he became more careless of his ward – and the Countess and Julia escaped from him – After his conduct to his son – they trembled lest in some act of despair he should on some future occasion equal the past scene, which *chilled them with horror* — The Countess was seized with the small-pox, which altered her features considerably, without impairing her beauty; this circumstance facilitated their eluding all search after them from the Duke, as Julia wore men's clothes; and they supported themselves by the sale of jewels.

The intelligent reader now perceives, that Mademoiselle Querci and her brother, were no other than the Countess de Sons and Julia, whom Lord Munster had met at Venice.

When the Duke de Salis retired to La-Trappe, the Countess de Sons appeared, and took possession of her fortune. She had remained constantly and sincerely attached to Lord Munster was flattered by his attentions at Venice, and found her esteem increased by the regard he paid to his pre engagements; but would not at that time discover herself, fearing that she only flattered herself that he saw her with the eyes of affection, and lest the small-pox had made *such* an alteration, as might change his

---

*Admiral Byng; on which occasion the following verses were made, which I now present to the reader.

> We the court-martial now begin to sicken,
> And find at last that we are conscience stricken.
> Sad suppliants in Byng's behalf we come,
> And humbly crave you would defer his doom!
> Bound by our oath, we cannot yet make clear
> What 'twas we meant, nor *never* shall, we fear.
> We found him guilty, and we found him not;
> We wish'd him sav'd, yet wish'd him to be shot.
> But as at land, so did we find at sea:
> If we did one, the other could not be.
> Save him, great chief – your royal mercy show!
> Shoot him, dread chief – let royal justice flow!
> Relieve our consciences with pitying eye,
> And grant that Byng may neither live nor die!

sentiments. Upon the Marquis de Villeroy's arrival in Italy, she was highly charmed to receive a letter from Lord Munster addressed to Mademoiselle de Querci, and determined to accompany him and Julia to England; but this was carefully concealed, to render the discovery more pleasing.

In the mean time, the family at Munster-house passed their time most agreeably, though Lord Munster, Sir Harry Bingley, and Mrs Lee, (who knew nothing of Mr Villars) often were melancholy and *distrait*.

Lord Munster made great preparations to celebrate the anniversary of Lady Darnley's wedding-day: on which occasion a number of buildings were added to those already mentioned on the pleasure-grounds — As all the best artificers were on the spot, these were executed in the ablest manner. One temple he finished without the inspection of any one.

On the morning of the masquerade, walking out with Sir Harry Bingley, he told him he should be glad to have his opinion of it. In this temple was painted the *cataract* of the river Dahl, which he had drawn on the spot* – the cottage where Miss Harris resided – and herself at work, in the same way in which he saw her, with her lovely boy playing beside her (Miss Harris had permitted Lord Munster to draw her picture, and he had fortunately taken an exact likeness) — Sir Harry Bingley started at beholding it, and exclaimed, 'It is her, it is, by Heaven, it is her! What artist drew the picture? it is, it is herself!' – he then sunk almost motionless in a chair! – Lord Munster carelessly answered – 'Bingley, are you mad? That picture *cannot* concern you; I painted it from life! Where did you see her? Answer but that question, and I am gone, gone that instant; the world should not detain me!' 'It is, it is, my Lord, the lovely woman I told you of. But her graces were yet more charming still than her beauty! an external glare of beauty may *captivte the eye, and ravish the sight*; but it is the graces that win the heart, that powerfully attract every faculty of a kindred mind! – I loved her, and was beloved! She loved my person, not my fortune. Her tenderness, her affection were my only joy!' 'Why then, replied Lord Munster, did you leave her? but make yourself easy on her account; she can be nothing to you; I expect her soon in England.' — 'In England!' — 'Yes, Sir,

* See Vol. II. Page 52.

in England, I fancy by this time she is married to my friend Ogilby.' 'Lord Ogilby!' 'Yes; he was passionately in love with her: she absolutely refused him; but it is not likely, possessing such beauty, such perfections – slighted by the author of her exclusion from every dear and valuable claim in society, relations, friends, reputation, and protection – that she should continue deaf to the earnest solicitations of *another*, who can restore her to these advantages – such a man as Ogilby, a tender lover, who would sacrifice his time and fortune to her, and who promised he would be *a father to her boy*.'

Sir Henry's senses appeared suspended. – He at last repeated, 'Distraction, madness, fury! But, by the great God of Heaven – he shall not be a *father to my boy!*' The agitation of his spirits rendered him almost unintelligible: Lord Munster could only understand that he intended to set out directly – he therefore dissuaded him from it – telling him, that if he refused staying that day (on which he meant to mark his respect to Lady Darnley) that he must renounce his friendship for ever! 'My Lord, returned he, I honor, I love you; your virtues demand the first, your amiable engaging qualities the last; but were you God instead of man you should not detain me! – A few hours may render her the wife of the happy Ogilby! There is damnation in that thought!' – As Lord Munster had contrived an agreeable surprise to Sir Henry – and Miss Harris and her child were actually arrived, and concealed at Mr Burt's, who had taken a separate house, for retirement, – it was necessary he should detain him; and as he had forgot to ask where there scene represented *was*, he availed himself of that circumstance, saying, 'Since, Sir, I cannot command your *complaisance*, I may at least enforce your *obedience*, for you know not *where* to go, without I tell you – and my lips shall be sealed up *for ever*, unless you pass this night here – If in the morning you choose to set off, I will instruct you in every particular. In the time Lord Munster was enjoying Sir Harry's happiness – some of his friends were equally engaged for him. The Countess de Sons and Julia, the Marquis de Villeroy, Mr Villars, and Mr Worthy, came to London before the masquerade – Mr Villars wrote to Lord Darnley, acquainting him privately with their arrival, and it was agreed in return they should all make their appearance on that occasion.

This entertainment was executed equal to the munificence and taste of Lord Munster – and as it was given entirely in honor of

Lady Darnley, the principal objects in his arrangements had a reference to her. Never was parental affection more fondly evinced, never was filial gratitude more entire. – It has been already observed, that nothing was ever more elegantly planned than Munster Village, the farm adjoining, and the pleasure-grounds which lead to the house: in the farm you wandered from variety to variety; buildings of great utility and much fancy, groves inspiring different sensations, from the lucid summits that wake the mind to gaiety, to the dark brown or *clair obscure* of trees crowding their branches together in the vale, which possess the soul with home-felt contemplation.

Above three hundred of the nobility and people of fashion in the neighbourhood were invited. Lord and Lady Darnley, Lord Munster, Lady Eliza, and Mr Worthy, were the only people unmarked. They received the company in the temple of Minerva, which faced a fine piece of water, on which there is an island. The river represented the Styx*, the island Elysium, and Charon ferried over passengers. His boat landing, the names of Demosthenes, Aristotle, Pindar, Plato, Apelles, Phidias, and Praxiteles, were announced to Lady Darnley – They were all dressed in Grecian habits. Demosthenes, in an elegant harangue, acquainted her, that the wise Minos had indulged them in their request, of taking that opportunity of doing homage to her superlative merit, and to return her thanks for reviving their memories in the encouragement she gave to the arts and sciences, as under her patronage the Muses had made Munster Village their capital seat. He then expatiated on the advantages she had procured to society – the influence of the philosophic spirit in humanizing the mind, and preparing it for intellectual exertion and delicate pleasures – in exploring, by the help of geometry, the system of the universe – in promoting navigation, agriculture, medicine, and moral and political science. Lady Darnley (though

* Elysium, Minos, Mercury, Charon, Styx, &c. are here necessarily introduced. If they should offend any pious or critical ears, I shall defend myself (as has been done before) by the solemn declaration which is always annexed by the Italian writers to works where they are obliged to use such expressions: '*Se havessi nomenato Fato, Fortuna, Destino, Elysio, Stigé, Etc. sono scarzi di penna poetica, non sentimenti di anema catolico.*' If I have annexed Fate, Fortune, Destiny, Elysium, Styx, &c. they are only the sports of a poetical fancy, not the sentiments of a Catholic mind.

totally unprepared, being ignorant of her nephew's plans) made a very ready and polite answer, returning them thanks for the honor they did her, which (she said) as it could afford them no other *pleasure*, than that of *obliging*, rendered the obligation greater. Demosthenes replied, that great geniuses are always superior to their own abilities.

Some time after Charon was observed to land some passengers in Roman habits; they proved to be Cicero, Lucretius, Livy, Virgil, Horace, Ovid, Varro, Tibullus, and Vitruvius. Cicero advancing, made Lady Darnley a speech similar to that of Demosthenes – as like thoughts will be ever born of the like subjects, by people who live in corresponding periods of the *progression of manners*. In such cases some considerable *similarity* of expression may be occasioned by the agency of *general principles*. Lady Darnley made a gracious reply, intimating her small merit, and the apprehensions she felt that physical causes might impede her good intentions; that her powers had been limited; but that she was far from thinking with Boileau, that wherever there is a Mæccenas, a Virgil or an Horace will arise, (curtsying to these gentlemen.) Cicero observed to her the happiness she enjoyed in living at a *period* distinguished by men of such shining abilities in every department!

Lady Darnley answered, that he honored her countrymen very much: that she acknowledged we have at present very able men in every department; but that in morality she was afraid we have refined more upon the *vices* of the ancients than *their virtues*, and she could not help questioning whether there was any minister, magistrate, or lawyer, now in Europe, who could explain the discoveries of Newton, or the ideas of Leibnitz, in the same manner as the principles of Zeno, Plato, and Epicurus, had been illustrated at Rome*.

He thanked her for her polite compliment, and retired with his companions.

They were succeeded by Italians, who were announced Lawrence de Medicis, Michael Angelo, Raphael, Titian, Ariosto, and Tasso. Lawrence de Medicis expressed his happiness from having been permitted the honor of paying his respects to her, and admiring the works of her creation, and complimented her in the

* By Cicero.

name of his friends for the encouragement she had afforded the arts. – She said, the applause of the worthy is too valuable to be received with indifference; but still modestly declined the praises bestowed on her, saying, she had endeavoured to follow *his* example, although the imitation was *a faint one*; and that the only commendation she aspired to was from *the attempt*. That without her assistance, she made no doubt, if physical causes did not prevent it*, that the society for the encouragement of arts, manufactures, and commerce in London, is well calculated to diffuse a spirit of taste in this nation – a society, which, without neglecting what tends more immediately to the improvement of agriculture, and the necessary arts of life, gives the most honorable encouragement to those which are elegant and ornamental. Had such a society been instituted fifty years ago, London, perhaps by this time, would have been the grand seat of the arts, as it is the envied seat of freedom.

Michael Angelo, that celebrated restorer of the arts of painting, sculpture, and architecture, expressed how infinitely he was charmed with Munster Village†. – 'What is really beautiful, said he, does not depend either upon fashion, or times; there may be *different ways* of expressing things in different ages; but there can only *be one* of conceiving them properly.' The temple, in which they were, was adorned with the paintings of Raphael‡, copied by an able artist. Lady Darnley, pointing to these, (and addressing him) said 'There is proof how much we fall short, how faintly we copy originals!' – Raphael replied, that her ladyship did him much honor; the pieces she had selected, had met with the suffrage of the public; but that, in his own acceptation, *the cartoons* were the best of his performances – which he apprehended a juster prevailing taste at present condemned: Otherwise the father of his people, approved of by Minos – so good so indulgent a prince to

---

* According to the Abbé de Bos's hypothesis.

† Those in the shades are supposed acquainted with the transactions in the world.

‡ The pictures were, the Parnassus of Raphael – and the school of Athens, which is a most glorious performance, and worthy the hand of a divinity – The first is in the hall of Constantine at Rome, and contains no less than twenty-eight figures – two of which in particular, the one representing Justice, and the other Meekness, are incomparable – They were the last things he executed before his death – They contain all that is excellent in painting, whether we consider them in the beauty of the composition, the noble gracefulness of the characters, the uncommon greatness of the style of the draperies, or the wonderful force of colouring, light, and shade.

his subjects – would not lock them up from public observations. – Lady Darnley was here quite at a loss; she blushed, hesitated, unwilling either to refuse her sovereign *taste* or *philanthropy!*

Lawrence de Medicis perceiving her situation, in pity of her confusion, retired with his company.

Charon again landed a groupe of figures; their dress declared them English, of the reign of King Charles II – They proved to be the Duke of Buckingham*, Sir William Petty, Mr Dryden, Mr Locke, Mr Waller etc. The Duke addressed Lady Darnley with that polite address peculiar to himself in his age, and which has since been sedulously studied, to the prevention of qualities which it should only be the harbinger of – he expatiated on her merit; that she had obliged the whole nation, as every one individual might receive improvement or pleasure by her means. – Lady Darnley returned him a most gracious answer, still intimating her apprehensions, that the arts perhaps were not likely to thrive in this soil, where our pursuits, opinions, and inclinations, vary with the weather – that the declension of letters after the reign of Charles II. but too fully justified her opinion. – The Duke answered her, that indeed that was the common and received opinion, and that the reign she mentioned was the Augustan age in England; but that he had the honor to assure her, that a just taste was by no means then formed. – The progress of philological learning, and the *Belles Lettres* was obstructed by the institution of the Royal Society, which turned the thoughts of men of genius to physical inquiries. – To that body we were indebted for the discoveries relating to light, the principle of gravitation, the motion of the fixed stars, the geometry of transcidental qualities; but that it was left to her ladyship to revive the agreeable arts, for which her name must be handed down to posterity with honor.

The following dialogue ensued between Charon and a Beau.

Beau. — I have seen all parts of the world, and should like to take a view of Elysium, being rather tired of this side of the Styx.

---

* He was sent over as Ambassador extraordinary to France on the King's restoration. He was received at that court with great distinction; which seldom considers more than the external appearance. His Grace possessed *all the graces*. Lewis XIV, then in the flower of his age, said he was the only *English* gentleman he had ever seen.

*Mercury to Charon. — He is too frivolous an animal to present to the wife Minos!

Charon. — Minos, Sir, knows nothing of *the graces* – but if you please I will row you to the infernal regions.

Beau. — With all my heart, I believe I shall meet more people of fashion there†; but, good master Charon, in what way shall I pass my time?

Charon. — If you are fond of doing nothing (a favourite passion with many fine gentlemen) Theseus will readily resign his seat to you: or if it is your genius, like many others, to choose to be,

> '*Though without business, yet in full employ,*'

you may join Sisyphus, or accompany the Danaides.

Beau. — Neither of these will suit me; *idleness* is *insipid*, and I *detest business!* But are there no public places?

Charon. — O! yes; great variety: each person in that place pursues those inclinations, whereby he had been swayed, or had rendered himself remarkable here on earth.

Beau. — There are fine women then, of course?

Charon. — As to women, no seraglio in the world comes up to it; as a part of whatever the world, since its creation, has ever yet produced, of lovely and enchanting amongst women are there assembled. – There you may view and gaze, with admiration, upon Helen, whose bewitching charms were so destructive to the family, the city, and the empire of King Priam. – On each side of her are Galatea, and Bressis, Lais, Phryne, and thousands more – There also you may behold in all their charms, in the full lustre of attraction, and decked in every grace, some of those happy fair-ones, whom the greatest poets, so lavish in their praise, have in their lays immortalised; such, amongst many others, are the Corinna of Ovid, the Lydia of Horace, the Lesbia of Catullus, the Delia of Tibullus, the Licoris of Gallus, and the Cynthia of Propertius.

Beau. — I will go; I am enchanted with the idea of seeing these *dear creatures*. – But I will shiver the wheel and distaff of the Destinies against the wall, and spoil their housewifery – I'll

---

* Deities interfere when they please – unseen by mortals!
† I Corinthians chap. i. v. 26.

take their spindle, where hang the threads of human life like beams driven from the sun, and mix them all together, kings and beggars! But hark'ee, master Charon, is there good music? I cannot do well without music!

Charon. — There are all kinds of concerto's and opera's, both vocal and instrumental, executed by the very *best* of the Italians, and the most celebrated voices from every part of the world. There are various pieces performed in all languages, and in all kinds of taste, for the universal satisfaction of the audience. Those who have a taste for ancient music, will be more gratified than they can be in Tottenham-street*. They will hear with admiration the gentle flute of Marsius, be ravished with the thorough-bass of Stentor, and expire with delight at the thrilling note of Misurus's trumpet.

Beau. — All this is charming; but what sort of a table is kept? One cannot altogether live on *love* and *music*; though one must *languish* and *expire* without them, as well *as with them!*

Charon. — If you are fond of good cheer, you have nothing to do but to pay a visit to Tantalus. Are you thirsty? The Styx, the Cocytus, and the Phlegethon present their waves to your acceptance.

Beau. — I should indeed rather prefer the nectar of the Gods – but as I shall not stay long (for I make it a rule never to stay long in a place) water may suffice!

Charon. — It would have been as easy to have escaped from the Labyrinth of Dædalus, as the infernal regions!

Beau. — I have always (though as wild as March, and inconstant as April) been a favourite with the fair! Ariadne procured for her Theseus a means of escape.

Charon. — I make no doubt, from your conversation, that you are not only the favourite, but the blessed Adonis of all the women: but *that* will avail you nothing. Lucifer, the unpitying Lucifer, though you should promise to offer him every day three hundred bulls in sacrifice†, would not lend you even one of the smallest of his imps to help you to get out.

Beau. — Did not Hercules escape from it, and carry Cerberus along with him? Did not Æneas (with the assistance of

* A concert established there in 1776.
† Horace, lib. ii. ode 14.

the golden bough, and led by the Cumæan Sybil) take the same journey to pay a visit to his father? Why may not I, like Orpheus, go to visit it while living?

Charon. — Orpheus was particularly indulged, and Eurydice restored to him on account of his charming voice, and the delightful music of his lyre! You have no such pretensions. But Alecto, Megara, and Tysiphone, will receive you graciously and open the gates of *Tartarus* to you. The least of your exploits will entitle you to their attentions:— they are too good, too reasonable, too indulgent to require from you the very great pains you have taken, through the whole course of your life, to rccommend yourself to them.

Beau. — Let us go then, old boy! I will try what a little flattery wil do with them! I can *say with Cæsar*, I wonder what fear is! – (Aside) But my heart plaguily misgives me for *all that!* but in my circumstances I must change for the better; my money is gone; and as I never gamed, I cannot expect the *club, or the waiters at the club*, to make *a subscription for me!*

Two peers and a baronet applied to Charon, to ferry them over to Munster-house: but Mercury again interfered, telling Lord C———d that although he had been thought in the world not to have been *sans quelque goût* in the *belle maniere*, and had been an encourager of the *Belles Lettres*, yet as Minos only permitted them to come back to the world (in the present case) to do honor to superlative feminine merit, none but such who had paid a proper respect to the sex in their life-time could be indulged in that pleasure. But if he would burn his book (wherein he depreciates women, and considers them only as the toys of dalliance) in *the fiery billows of Phlegethon*, he would intercede for him with Minos. This the peer rejecting, his brother the baronet intreated to be permitted to go in his stead; but Mercury reminded him, he had pulled down a house built by Inigo Jones, and therefore could have no pretensions to taste!

Lord L———n was ferried over by himself; and after paying his compliments to Lady Darnley, returned; when the following dialogue took place in Elysium between his lordship, and the other peer above mentioned.

Lord C———d.——— Your lordship may believe that I could have no great pleasure in seeing a woman's follies: I was only desirous of inquiring what they are doing at home, or in America? Did I desire to punish an enemy in the severest manner, I would inflict nothing worse upon him than to oblige him to listen to all the follies in which he has no share, and to be witness to gaieties in which he cannot partake. My heart was never dilated by the amplitude of generous principles; nothing was ever interesting to me, but in proportion as it contributed to my *own* particular *gratifications*. Curiosity now however prevailed with me to attempt going to discover in what way they are going on, being apprehensive of the consequences of the measures formerly adopted. Whoever would deprive men of their natural rights, is an enemy to the race of men; and he that thinks it can be effectuated without universal mischief, is a stranger to the ways of Providence; the most invariable rule of which is, That nothing contradictory to its original laws shall ever be accomplished, either of a physical or moral nature, without bringing ruin on that people which has instituted it. How few are capable of distinguishing the good and pernicious effects which will follow the instituting a new law, before it is enacted! To remedy present evils, they make a law which brings greater mischiefs along with it, though imperceptible to their shallow capacities. No two understandings on earth are more different than a judicial and legislative; many men enjoy the first, who have not the least emanation of the second. When a law is to be founded, which depends on the first principles in human nature, there genius only can effectuate any discovery of truth; the mind must dart forward into futurity, from the principles which it knows in human nature: a genius of quite a different kind from that of distinguishing between right and wrong in any particular case. The first only can form the legislator, and plan laws of utility and public good, the latter decide of the consequences of them when they are made. The one capacity is the most rare, most excellent and beneficial blessing bestowed on man; the other to be found in almost all mankind, or attainable by habit, yet useful when confined to its proper sphere of action, and not permitted to rove, with the imagination of the superior *few*, amongst the regions of exalted genius.

Lord L———n.——— It is not enough, my Lord, that the English are a *miserable*, they render themselves a *ridiculous* people: And, after all the noise the brawlers make in the lower house, they only fight the battles, aid the wishes of the Americans, and exalt the triumph of the French! In private life it is reckoned a good expedient, for the sake of an easy, quiet life, to be patient and submissive under what are supposed *necessary evils*: but I differ so much from this maxim, that I am convinced those will ever be *trod upon* who *creep*; and that certain submissions derogatory to a sense of honor in an individual or the nation, never *prevent the blow*, though it may be *protracted* for a reason, in order to lay it on with a redoubled force at a time our strength is weakened, and that we are debilitated by our mortifications and a sense of the submissions we have made injurious to the honor of an individual or the pride of the nation. It is a mortifying area, but must have its place in the annals of this disgraced kingdom, whilst extravagance and every species of gaieties daily increase.

I am sorry to acquaint your Lordship, that the publication of your book has given in England the same wound to morality and business as the publication of *the spirit of laws* has given in France to the monarchical constitution. The English study nothing now but the *Graces*. Procrastination is the *ton*, because any thing *abrupt is ungraceful*. The increase of manners has always been thought as imperceptible as the hand of a clock, which though in constant motion cannot be distinguished in *that motion*. But your book has occasioned a more rapid change: your countrymen having exchanged the *armour of Mars* for the *amours of Venus*, their *greatness of mind* and *magnanimity* for *trifling pursuits*; and, instead of speaking forcibly in the senate, they whine a tale of love in the ear of their mistresses: having descended suddenly, like skilful musicians, from the *forte* and the *pomposo* to the *pia* and the *pianissimo*. Refinement will bring us back to barbarity — far be it from me to suppose such an event can happen suddenly; but in the course of a few years, I make no doubt, as a man in days of yore that could read *had the benefit of clergy*, so will a man be esteemed an able minister, or an expert negotiator of business, if he can write a pretty sonnet – or dance a good minuet.

Lord C———d.——— The graces, my lord, I still say, the graces for ever – and as to dancing, can there be any science more useful for a minister to learn – to figure *out* with a good grace, never to *lose time*, and not even to nod, instead of *sleeping a century?**

---

* Alludes to a circumstance that passed in the house of commons.

Two other passengers applied to Charon to ferry them over the Styx, Homer and Ossian.

Mercury told Charon that he might carry Homer to Olympus, and place him with the Demigods; but he could not be permitted to go to Munster-house, for the same reason Lord C———d had been rejected: But Ossian had a just claim to that indulgence.

The Chief of other years being landed, addressed Lady Darnley as follows:

Ossian. ——— I have escaped from *the narrow-house*!* I have crossed *Col-amon*†, O daughter of Munster, to behold thy glory. My joy returns as when I first beheld the maid, the white-bosomed daughter of strangers, *Moina*‡ with the dark blue eyes: But *Crimionaϰ* should be thy name, for thou art the guiding star of the women of Albion, who mark no years with their deeds! Time rolls on, seasons return, but they are still unknown. Vanity is their recompence; and when their years shall have an end, no grey stone shall rise to their renown! But the departure of thy soul shall be a stream of light! A thousand bards shall sing of thy praise; and the maids of harmony, with their trembling harps, shall relate thy mighty deeds!

Thy son, when the years of his youth shall arise, will raise the mould about thy stone, and bid it speak to other years! The joy of his grief will be great! Like the memory of joys that are past, pleasant and mournful to the soul. He will say, 'she will not come forth in her beauty, will move no more in the steps of her loveliness: but she will be like the rainbow on streams, or the gilding of sun-beams on the hills! She has not fallen unknown! Her fame surrounded her like light; her rays, like those of the sun, cherished all on whom they fell. Her wealth was the support of the needy; the weak rested secure in her halls! She softened at the sight of the sad; her blue eyes rolled in tears for the afflicted; her breast of snow heaved for the oppressed; and the moving of her lips assuaged their grief! – O sons of Albion, may you behold her son, like the *halo* of the *rainbow*, exhibit *the same* though *fainter colours!'*

---

* *The narrow-house*, the grave.

† *Col-amon*, a narrow river.

‡ *Moina*, a woman soft in temper.

ϰ *Crimona*, a woman with a great soul.

Lady Darnley. — Father of heroes, dweller of eddying winds, thy praise gladdens my heart! My soul is exalted, my fame secured, by the voice of Conna*! Thou hast been a beam of light to latter times, as they mighty deeds have been remembered, though though hast long been a blast!

Thy renown grew only on the fall of the haughty; thy foes were the sons of the guilty; but thine arms rescued the feeble!

Thou wentest forth in echoing steel, and conquered the king of many isles: He brought thee his daughter Oina-moral, as an offering of peace. She was gentle as the evening breeze; her hair was of a raven black, and her bosom vied in whiteness with the *Canna*† on the Fuar-Bhean‡. — And though thy locks were young, yielded her to the hero she loved✧! But like unto Cathmor★ of old, I perceive the sound of thy praises is displeasing to thine ear!

Ossian. — Just praise, like the water of a *clear fountain*, was ever pleasant to my taste; but I never rejoiced in unmerited applause, resigning that *muddy joy* to the sons of later days!

It is true, O daughter of Albion, that, surrounded by the valiant in arms, I conquered the king of many isles — that he presented the maid to me in her loveliness as an offering of peace! She purpled the morn with blushes as she approached, and scattered such bright rays, as the sun might have dressed his beams with for that day's glory! But she had given her heart to another, and met my eyes of love with sorrow! In thrilling notes vibrating from her inmost soul, she conveyed to me the pangs of her heart! 'Breaker of the shield (said she) give ear unto the voice of mourning, attend to my tale, of woe — a tale,

---

* Ossian is sometimes poetically called Conna.

† *Canna*, a sort of down, like, but whiter and shorter than cotton; it is very common on the hills of the highlands. They have attempted to spin it, but it was either too short, or the fingers that made the experiment too indelicate — Nothing can exceed the purity of is whiteness.

‡ *Fuar-Bhean*, cold mountains.

✧ Livy has justly raised the praise of Scipio, who restored to her lover the Celtiberian captive; which has been the favourite topic of eloquence in every age and every country. The author cannot think it merited such commendation, as to have acted otherwise would have been mere brutality — but if granted so liberally to Scipio, it cannot be refused to Ossian.

★ Cathmor is represented in Ossian's poems, as lying down beside a river to have the sound of his praises lost in that of a water-fall.

which though thy eyes of steel are used more to strike fire than shed a tear, must have that power to move thee.'

My parents had seen many returning seasons with their springs, but no offspring of theirs arose. My mother lamented a disgrace, scarce known amongst the daughters of Caledonia. She consulted the cunning-man of the rock: He said, 'Daughter, be of good cheer; take the son of thine adversary that is low, rear him; thy piety will be rewarded; thou shalt have a daughter whom thou *must give him to wife!*' When she declared this unto my father (as she was stricken in years) there immediately ran a smile over his face, like the little ruffling of water when a gentle breeze breathes upon the surface of a lake; but he adopted Tonthormid, and some moons after I came forth as a flower; but as the bud, hit with an envious worm ere he can spread his sweet leaves to the air, or dedicate his beauty to the sun, dies, so shall I soon fly away as a shadow. Not the white down that decks the silver swan is more unlike the sooty raven's back, than my lover from the rest of his sex. Bred up with him, my first accents were attuned to love; he took delight in my infantine caresses. Time ran on with its years – My father corrected my tenderness; and I became sensible of my error as soon as I was conscious of my feelings. Tonthormid also, from our inequality of fortune, tried to suppress his passion, judging what was then a lambent fire, would soon blaze into a flame! True love, like the lily of the vale, is fond of concealment; but, as the fragrancy of the one occasions its discovery, so does the concealment of the other prove its reality! I loved and was beloved; my father saw, and approved our passion. A succession of moons had not frozen the genial current of his soul, nor repeated shocks blunted all its tenderest sensations – But we were ignorant of his intentions. When he appointed us to meet him at his cave of contemplation, the heart of Tonthormid palpitated with fear, mine with hope – we had a considerable way to go, but *remained silent!* — we walked through a pleasant grassy walk, shaded with rows of lime-trees, at the side of which ran along, in plaintive murmurs, a crystal brook, on the side of whose mazy and translucent stream were planted bushes of various kinds, with birds in high harmony on the sprays.

Arrived at the cave, my father announced to my lover that he must prepare to accompany him to battle! Aghast he stood, silent as the midnight hour, unmoved as the statue of despair! The venerable Chief reproached him for his coldness.

'Alas! said he, the din of arms is no more offensive to my ear than the murmuring of falling waters, the vernal breeze sighing through the leaves, or the melodious song of the evening nightingale; but if we should fall in battle, what will become of this lovely maid?'

My father, swearing by the great Loda, promised I should be his – if we conquered – but reminded him, that

'Love should be the zephyr, not the whirlwind of the soul!'

Tonthormid was all rapture, while every line in my countenance, witnessed my satisfaction. We were restored to that unexpected tranquility of spirits, which naturally follows a great dejection in most minds, when the first pangs are somewhat abated – not unlike that stillness in the sky which is sometimes observed when two opposite and gentle winds have just overcome one another's motion – or like the tide at the moment of high water, before it has received the contrary direction.

They set out, receiving my caresses, intermixed with smiles and tears, like an April sun shining through transient showers. They met the foe, *conquered*, and *returned*.

The feast of shells was prepared, the maids of mirth attended with their harps, and the rising sun would have beheld me Tonthormid's! The virgins envied me in the hall, my steps were strewed with flowers, and I was happiest, where a thousand are happy. The subtile air was calm from mists, and water with her curled waves swept the bounded channels of the deep; the nightingales were heard in the grove, and soothed my soul with tender tales of love; not a breeze breathed through the trees; all nature was still, as if it paid homage to our passion. But oh! my summer's day was soon turned into winter's night! Ah, soul ambition! which like water-floods, not channel bound, dost neighbours overrun! – fell violence leaped forth like thunder wrapped in a ball of fire! Thou camest with thy men of steel; I beheld thee from the clefts of the rock; terrors turned upon me, like an earthquake they shook my trembling heart! they still pursue my soul as the wind. My joy is withered; my welfare has passed away like a cloud; my comforts have been like winter suns, that rise late and set betimes, set with thick clouds, that hide their light at noon!'

Thus sang the maid in her grief, like the *Lus-cromicina*, bending in pensive silence, a beautiful flower drooping in the shade, wanting the beams of the sun to revive it. She soon perceived my heart was not made of brass, or carved from the stony rock. Hope animated her weakened spirits, whilst the dignity of her soul irradiated every feature; the blush of modesty stole over the cheek, and the graces dwelt on her coral lips. Sweet as the dew from heaven her lovely accents fell, and moved me. She proceeded, 'I see my tears have mollified thy heart! If fame tells true, never over the fallen did thine eyes rejoice, and thou knowest the herbs on the hill!* Restore me then to the hero that is low; my tears will refresh him, as the dew of the morning doth the green herbage! – He mocked at fear; never retired from the foe, or was ever vanquished, but by the son of Fingal! Glorious is it to thee, O hero! great will be thy renown; thou hast subdued the first of men!

Were the earth his bed, a rock his pillow, his curtain heaven, with him alone could I be blessed! From a rock that weeps a running crystal, I will fill his shell cup. I'll gently raise his weakened body†, and the murmur of this water, instead of music, shall charm him into sleep; and whilst he sleeps my cares shall watch to preserve him from the beast of prey! The fern on the heath, if cut a thousand times, represents the same figure – so is the image of my love engraved on the inmost core of my heart! I hold the *thread* of his peace: can I forget its delicate texture, or that it is warped with *those* of his heart? I could grow to my hero like ivy; but like the aspenleaf I tremble, like the sensitive plant I shrink back at thy approach! Thou mayest swim against the stream with a crab, feed against the wind with the deer, but thou canst never possess my heart! Love for him, or grief, are the only passions that can fill the heart of Oinamoral! But thou mayest go forth in echoing steel and increase thy glory – or the hearts of a thousand other virgins, will beat an unison to thy sighs, and return thy passion!'

---

* The Highlanders are peculiarly intelligent in understanding the virtue of plants in curing wounds – The regularity of their lives precludes all diseases, such as are incident to old age excepted.

† Tonthormid was supposed wounded by Ossian.

Thus sung the daughter of many isles; her trembling harp was turned to mourning, and her lute into the voice of them that weep. My heart was never wrought of steel, nor hewn out of the rugged pebble; but she would have extracted honey out of the rock, and oil out of the flinty rock! My heart was *tender*, though my *arm was strong!* I resigned her to the man of her soul! But I had the supreme delight of exhaling the falling tear from the cheek of beauty, as when the pearly dew on the surface of the narcissus, and the snow-drop evaporates at the kindly instance of the solar ray. Had I been deaf to her tale of woe, I should have merited a cold chill to extinguish my flame, as if a *thousand winters* contracted *into one*, scattered their snow and froze the very centre! No praises can be due for refraining from barbarity, unknown till the sons of refinement came into the world!

Lady Darnley. – A great mind is ever tenacious of even the shadow of a favor received, but loses the idea of a benefit conferred – In what way, O first of men! shall I welcome thy approach? Wilt thou partake of the feast of shells, or be honored with the dangers of the chase?

Ossian. — Chase was never to me such sport as the battle of the shields! But this is a tale of the times of old, the deeds of the days of other years; manners alter with times, as the earth by the seasons. Let the sons of Albion listen to the voice of Conna, 'Never search for battle, nor fear it when it comes.'

Ossian retired, and a hangman from the assizes told Lady Darnley, that she had ruined his trade; for, all the poor of the country-side being employed in manufactures, etc. they had no inducement to steal, theft being the necessary consequence of idleness*.

The hangman retired; and Lady Darnley was addressed by a few women in tattered robes. Making an apology for their dress, they said, it was her ladyship who had condemned them to those unseemly garbs. She inquired, In what way she was culpable to them? They answered, By not only promoting industry, which was highly detrimental to their interests, but also procuring by her munificence theatrical and other entertainments for man-

* In the years 1759 and 1760, when we were at war with France, there were but twenty-nine criminals who suffered at Tyburn. In the years 1770 and 1771, when we were at peace with all the world, the criminals condemned amounted to one hundred and fifty-one.

kind, which completed their misfortunes, as it rendered ineffectual their allurements:— that they might formerly (out of the profits of their industry) have purchased annuities, like other eminent personages in the age, and *lived comfortably* on the *distresses of others*; but that they had always too much conscience, and too great and generous souls for that:— that they were now reduced to the alternative of removing from that part of the country, or starving where they were; and, preferring the first to the last, they had determined to go to Birmingham, where, under the auspices of the magistrates* of that place, they would have a good chance of succeeding in their profession; as it had always been found that recreations of some kind are necessary, and that if innocent amusements were denied, mankind would have recourse to the other.

The Goddess of Folly, with her cap and bells, approached Lady Darnley; who, smiling, asked her what had procured her the honor of her company? She answered, That being excluded at all other times from these regions, it induced her to come then, where she flattered herself, for one night in her life, not to be ridiculed; as it is only Absurdity that laughs at Folly. Her ladyship replied, That none indeed were entitled to smile at another's weakness, who are conscious of their own.

Miss Bingley, by her aunt's request, was in the character of a pastoral shepherdess, and affected to by vastly coy, and a great huntress. She said she wielded the crook and the javelin with equal dexterity; and that though she was terrified at the voice or appearance of a lover, yet she made nothing of lopping off the head of a wild boar, or of thrusting a spear into the jaws of a lion. She was pursued by (James Mordaunt as) a pastoral lover. Lady Darnley told her that such swains are mighty good-natured, and never do any mischief to any *but themselves*; a leap from a rock, or a plunge into a river, being their usual catastrophe.

Lord Munster walked away with Sir Harry Bingley, and shewed him, on one of the back grounds a cottage similar to that represented in the temple above-mentioned. They advanced, and saw Miss Harris, and her lovely boy playing at her feet. Sir Harry fixed his eyes, and with a peculiar wildness exclaimed, Sport not, my friend, with my sorrows! – Lord Munster assured him of the

* Who opposed a licensed theatre there last year.

reality; but he almost swooned away at the discovery, and was perfectly enchanted with his lovely boy. Every explanation taking place to their mutual satisfaction, Mr Burt being in the secret, and some more friends, the ceremony was immediately performed, and Miss Harris was introduced that very evening, as Lady Bingley, to the family at Munster-house.

Lord Munster, leaving this happy pair, joined Lord Sombre; two ladies pasied by them, one in a habit similiar to that Mademoiselle de Querci had wore at the masquerade at Venice: the other had assumed the figure of Diana. Struck with their majestic appearance, they followed them. The mask of the latter dropped, as if ashamed to conceal so much beauty. Lord Sombre stooping, instantly restored to her the *unfaithful* guardian of her charms. The lady, covered with that agreeable confusion inherent to the sex, apologized for the trouble she had given him! He replied, he could not but acknowledge that it was a trouble to him to be the instrument of depriving the company of the sight of so much beauty. That, Sir, replied she, may be your opinion; but my intention is to see, and *not be seen*. But a lady, replied his lordship, who represents Diana, would appear more in character if she could consent not *to be concealed*, nor to hide those beams of brightness which were designed to be the light of the world. Sir, said she, if I must support my character, it is not at all the less in my power because my mask is on, being still the moon though in eclipse – but my intention of appearing in the character of Diana, was to keep Actæon at a distance.

In the mean time Lord Munster had neither seen or heard the above conversation, the whole powers of his soul being absorbed in attention to the lady first mentioned. But what were his emotions, when he knew the well known voice of Mademoiselle de Querci! She told him, that she believed he was the gentleman who was still denominated at Venice *Il Febo del Inghilterra!* He told her, it was impossible he could have any pretensions to so flattering a distinction; but intreated to know whether he could believe that he had the happiness of addressing the woman he adored, whom from motives of honor he had been induced to suppress his passion for, but which scruples on his part he had been relieved from since that period? Mademoiselle de Querci (for it was she herself) answered, that every apology he could make for his infidelity to the Countess de Sons, would only lessen him in her esteem, as, to her certain knowledge, she was still single, and fondly attached to him. Had it been otherwise (said she) my Lord, I should have cheerfully *consented* to what I must now refuse, as I never will act in opposition to the interest of the Countess. Lord Munster, flattered at her coming to Munster-house, asked if she was perfectly sincere in the favourable hint she had given him – that nothing but his pre-engagement would have prevented her from according herself to his wishes? She answered, I desire, my Lord, you'll not judge me by your country-women; for, from what I have heard of their characters, there is no well-bred woman who ever makes any pretensions to *sincerity*. Does not every body say what they do not mean, and promise what they never intend to perform? and yet all of them, to a single woman, will compliment the justness of your remarks. – In Italy we are more sincere; and I now have the honor to assure you, that nothing at present occupies my thoughts, or interests me equal to your fulfilling of your engagements with the Countess de Sons, whose constancy for you demands on your part every return. In saying this, a sigh escaped Mademoiselle de Querci, which took refuge in Lord Munster's bosom – while her blushes raised hopes which her tongue denied confirming! Her lover felt a severe struggle between love and honor. — The most severe misfortune to a virtuous man is to be in such a state that he can hardly so act as to approve his own conduct. But his distraction was increased, in finding Mademoiselle de Querci had taken advantage of his *reverie* to retire, with a composure that decieved his vigilance, and an address which prevented his distrust. – He went every where in pursuit of her, but she eluded his search.

A magician with two enchanted knights addressed Lady Eliza, who (I have already observed) was dressed as a slave attending Mrs Worthy. He told her he would unfold her future fate, and, if she would retire to a place of privacy, he would convince her, and the queen she attended, that he was very well skilled in the science of astrology. Lord and Lady Darnley; Lord Sombre, Lord Munster, and Mrs Lee begged leave to accompany them. The two knights accompanied the magician, who he said must remain enchanted until they were released by the hands of their fair mistresses. After several magical incantations, he told Lady Eliza many things concerning the Marquis de Villeroi, and Mrs Lee of Mr Villars. But he astonished Lord Munster more particularly in telling him he was a *perplexed lover* – but assured him that he would be soon relieved from his anxiety; and that perhaps that very evening would terminate his adventures, and render all the present company joyful! Could you do this, replied Lord Munster, I would swear you had more wit than Mercury, or his son Autolycus, who was able to change black into white!

In the mean time two ladies appeared: They were majestic in their persons, and very magnificent in their apparel. The magician, addressing himself to the company, said, if it was agreeable, he would give them ocular proofs of his art. They answered, By all means! He then presented one of the enchanted knights to Lady Eliza, the other to Mrs Lee, and Lord Munster to one of the ladies who had just appeared (in the mean time Lord Darnley had prevented the admission of other company.) – He then desired them all to unmask. The agreeable discovery this produced is not easy to give an adequate idea of; as the magician was no other than Mr Worthy; the enchanted knights, the Marquis de Villeroi, and Mr Villars; and the Lady Mademoiselle de Querci. – Mr Worthy then, addressing Lord Munster, said, Your perplexity, my Lord, now ceases:— This Lady is the Countess de Sons (whose smiles confirmed her previous conversation with him that evening:) He made his suitable acknowledgments: whilst Lord Sombre was enchanted to discover, in the Countess's companion, his lovely Diana, who had changed her dress, and proved to be Julia, sister to the Marquis de Villeroi, and justly admired by all who saw her: Her shape was as fine as the statue of the Medician Venus, of as fine a complexion as the Leda of Corregio, with a sweetness of expression that would have made Guido paint no other face, if he had been alive.

The masquerade finished, which had afforded so much amusement, and conferred so much happiness on the parties. Lady Bingley was received by Lady Darnley with the utmost complacency. It is the imperfection of *human* goodness to make its conscious worth an argument of want of mercy to those that are deficient: but Lady Darnley had thoroughly studied the most useful of all sciences, human nature, and was ever ready to make allowances for its defects. She was the more attentive to Lady Bingley, on account of her peculiar situation; while in the effusions of her gratitude there was a dignity that commanded as much respect as if she had been conferring a favor beyond that she acknowledged. Her relations, who abandoned her in her adversity – when alone true friendship can prove its superiority over its shadow, *worldly civility* – were now eager to pay their compliments to her.

Mr Villars was the only person who appeared unhappy at this time. Mrs Lee had been hurt at never hearing from him since her husband's death, and was confirmed that his present appearance was occasioned more from a concurrence of circumstances than from his own particular desire or inclination. – It was in vain he urged, that his having absented himself from England was occasioned by her refusing to see him previous to her husband's death; which circumstance he had been unapprised of, previous to his meeting the Marquis de Villeroi at Paris. – She answered, That he had neither been a lover that had the tenderness, nor a friend that had the generosity to interest himself for her; though he must have been sensible of her partiality, from the pains she took to avoid him:— that, concerning the strange event that had occurred relative to her husband and him, she had never taken any pains to justify herself; and she thought people in general were to blame that did so; for satire is generally levelled against persons, not vices, as there are few who wish to punish what does not put them out of humour, and they make a personal affront the pretended defender of virtue. If a woman, therefore, would *preserve her character*, this is the effectual way *of losing it*, and if she has *none to preserve* she need not tell *all the world* so. – 'But (said she) as I must now decline your proffered hand, the offer of which does more honor to your generosity than the acceptance would to my prudence, I shall now disclose my sentiments to you without any disguise:— I was married to a man, whom I could not look up to with a consciousness of his superior understanding or worth; his treatment of me was injurious; my feelings I with difficulty suppressed: my quick apprehension of injury, and my partiality for you, made me indulge an inclination that aggravated to me the horrors of my situation. – I loved, and was utterly incapable of divesting myself of a passion, which, although often dangerous, is always delightful. – I was punished for my temerity; the calumny I met with, I justly incurred, from the appearance I had subjected myself to. When I parted from my husband, I would on no account see you – you went abroad; your caprice now brings you back; you judge it equitable, perhaps, to restore me to that world I relinquished on your account – but time has conquered my partiality, and, after my former experience in that state, I cannot help shuddering at a contract which nothing can dissolve but death. To me it is terrible to reflect, that it is a strangely unequal conflict, in which the man only ventures the loss of a few temporary pleasures, the woman the loss of liberty, and almost the privilege of opinion. – From the moment she's married she becomes the subject of an arbitrary lord; even her children, the mutual pledges of their affection, are absolutely in his power, and the law countenances him in the use of it – and a woman finds no redress for the indelicate abuses of an uncivil, a passionate, and avaricious, an inconstant, or even a drunken husband – from matrimonial decisions there is no appeal.' – Mr Villars said every thing to justify himself, adding, that the most candid mind will sometimes, under certain circumstances, deviate from itself; but it is the property *only* of narrow minds to persist in prejudice against conviction. – As the quarrels between lovers are the renewal of love – these differences were soon settled, agreeable to their mutual wishes.

Mr Burt testified great joy at the celebration of the nuptials of his grandson – That good man died the next day, without any complaint, with a smile of complacency on his venerable face. In an age where men of letters seem so regardless of morals – in an age where they have endeavoured to persuade mankind, with but too much success, that the virtues of the mind and of the heart are incompatible – let them cast their eyes on the character of Mr Burt – When they find so many virtues united in a man, whose understanding was both sublime and just – when they find a man of his penetration to have been a strictly moral man – they will then, perhaps, be convinced that vice is the natural effect of an imperfect understanding.